Boom-shacka-lacka

Stories

William Marquess

For Rebecca,
For all the years,
with love ——
Will

Fomite

Burlington, Vermont

The epigraph on page 8 is from the book *The Art of Fielding* by Chad Harbach. Copyright © 2011 by Chad Harbach. Reprinted by permission of Little, Brown and Company, New York NY. All rights reserved.

Five of these pieces ("Don't Fail Me Now," "Harold Goes to School," "Harold Goes Hip-Hop," and "Harold Does Not Go Gentle") first appeared in the *Onion River Review*.

ISBN-13: 978-1-942515-62-3
Library of Congress Control Number: 2016946772

Fomite
58 Peru Street
Burlington, VT 05401
www.fomitepress.com

Cover Art: "Great Blue Heron in Flight"
Photograph by Jonathan Sherrill

For Joel and Emily, friends nonpareil

Acknowledgments

Thanks to my parents, again; to my three dear siblings and their families; to Christina, Nat, Carey, Nick, Liz, Lorrie, Maura, Greg, Kerry, Kathie, Bob, Toni, Joan, Tim, George, and all my splendid colleagues; to John Reiss, John Engels, and Hank Moses; to Missy Holland; to David Huddle, Jonathan Sherrill, and Jasmine Lamb; to Linda Pardo; to Pascale and Benoit, Elaine, Alessandra, and Marina; to Farrah, Janet, Stephanie, and everyone in Hem-Onc; to Marc and Donna; to all Onionists everywhere; to the students who read these pieces when they were just SFDs; and to the people of Saint Michael's College, my long home.

Data shmata, tell me a story!

—Mugwump Toujours

Contents

Foreword   1

Don't Fail Me Now   8

The Snow Man Speaks   11

Boscoscuro Fleurdumal   33

What Would I Have to Give You?   51

The Harold Poems   69

But Seriously   91

Sometimes in the Night   111

Ultra-Boy and Marie   119

Make Me a Wreck as I Come Back   141

Oh! You Pretty Things   166

The Night the Washington Generals Won   187

Foreword

Dear Cancer: A Love Letter

April 2010

Dear Cancer,

Bear with me. I'm loaded with questions.

Why do I call you dear?

Because you could have killed me. And you still might. Because we must hold close the things we wrestle with most fiercely.

Because statistics baffle me. They say a person in my condition, Stage I lung cancer, has a 49% chance of living five years. Some people, they quickly add, live longer. Which must mean that some live not as long. Which am I?

Because I don't know what else to say. You found me at age fifty-five. Without you, I might have gone on living in relatively happy half-consciousness. I would have felt less pain. I would have known less love.

Why do we call you cancer?

Because you resemble the crab after which the constellation and zodiacal sign are named. You move sideways, in darkness, discreetly. Your claws clasp, and then you consume. You are nurtured by our bodies like all those bacteria we hear about living inside us but in which we don't really believe. When we are terrified by something that could kill us, we want to take names; we want to externalize the creature. This thing, this nodule, this growth, could not be part of me; it is crablike; it is cancer.

Why me?

The *New Yorker* cartoon gets this right. It shows a despairing half-dressed man sitting on an examining table. The doctor says, "Perhaps the more appropriate question is 'Why not you?'"

I had never been a smoker. I ate well and drank moderately. I throve on frequent exercise.

It turns out that ten to fifteen per cent of all lung cancers occur in non-smokers. Researchers have begun developing a whole category of non-smoker's lung cancer, with its own etiology and treatment. It has something to do with mutations in our DNA — which might as well be theoretical physics, for all I understand of it.

Still, the essential wisdom about avoiding it is "everything in moderation." So why me, moderate me? One friend said, "Will, you don't deserve this."

But why not me?

I was one of the lucky ones. I had already enjoyed many years of excellent health. And I found you, Cancer, in the best way: by accident. I had a stubborn cold; when it wouldn't let go, my physician suggested a chest x-ray, to see if it might be pneumonia; the x-ray showed that it was. And also a spot on my right lung that was, as they say, "concerning." There you were, glowing on the screen like a shiny marble in my lung. Cancer doesn't cause pain until it has grown so large that it is impeding other functions—and by then it's often too late. Thank God, or something, for pneumonia.

Why can't I just haul off and say "thank God"?

Because I'm not a believer. I don't question the faith of others—unless it moves them to hatred and violence. But I don't have faith myself, in any traditional sense. I understand God as a human invention—one of great power, worthy of study and awe, but an invention nonetheless. I am more at ease saying "thank the stars"—which may, of course, be just another way of saying "thank God." Or "thank the people who love me"—and many of them understand their love in terms of something they call God. Which is all right with me.

Samuel Johnson wrestled with his own fierce belief, but could not, in the end, surrender it. He could not conceive of dying without an afterlife. He quoted Shakespeare's *Measure for Measure* with horror: "Aye, but to die, and go we know not where,/To lie in cold obstruction, and to rot..." It was too much to fathom. There must be something else.

Perhaps there is. Perhaps there's some grand mutation that I'm shutting out because I will not give myself over to it. I am not prepared to say that Johnson was wrong. I just don't know, and to me it feels false to base my life (and my notion of death) on pretending that I do know. Possibly I'm wrong. But I'm wrong in a way that feels right to me.

Why do we fear you so?

Because Johnson was right. We spend a lifetime trying to avoid nothingness in all its forms — boredom, bankruptcy, ennui. Philip Larkin says, "Most things may never happen: this one will." Maybe we should take cheer in the universality of this condition, which applies equally to all races and classes and creeds. But how can we be comforted by what Larkin calls "total emptiness for ever"?

So we tried to excise you. A surgeon removed the part of my lung where you had made a home. He said it went well. He thought he "got it all."

In the cardiothoracic ward of the hospital, I was surrounded by older people. One night I overheard my roommate, Mr. Cutting, having a terrible time because he was so shrunken that the nurse could not find a vein in which to insert his IV. By the fourth day of my stay, when

I was strong enough to start walking in the hall, with my own IV trailing me on a wheeled pole, I saw that room after room in that ward was occupied by someone with white hair. For a moment, it made me feel young—and then I saw that I was one of them.

So how can this be a love letter?

Why would I want to declare my affection for this thing—for you, Cancer—that put me in that place, if only for a while? Because (to quote Johnson again) "Nothing focuses the mind like a hanging." Because being there, being here, makes me think again about what I want. In the fiction workshops that I teach, we always do an exercise based on the following fill-in-the-blank template, in which X is a character the writer is trying to develop.

X wants _____
But _____
So _____.

X wants to be here more fully, refusing the phony comforts of cliché. "Everything happens for a reason"? How can anyone believe that? What reason could possibly justify the Holocaust? "He's in a better place"? Who knows that? What place is better than a morning in April, or being loved?

X wants to live up to the generosity poured on him during the recent unpleasantness. Little, nameless, unremembered acts of kindness and of love. Cards, gifts, meals, visits and conversations, e-mails of support, students paying attention as if their lives depended on it. Dear Cancer, thank you. X didn't deserve this. But he accepts with gratitude.

So?

X wants to live as if this were always the case. Since it is.

> Dopo tanta
> nebbia
> a una
> a una
> si svelano
> le stelle.
>
> Respiro
> il fresco
> che mi lascia
> il colore
> del cielo.
>
> Mi riconosco
> immagine passeggera
> presa in un giro
> immortale.
>
> --Giuseppe Ungaretti

My Italian friend Marina sent me this poem when I was in the hospital. A rough prose translation: After so much fog, one by one the stars come out. I breathe in the freshness left to me by the color of the sky. I recognize myself as a fleeting image rapt in an immortal turning.

Dear Cancer, stay well. Stay out. Keep in touch.

                                                            June 2015

P. S.

Hey, Cancer, five years have passed. Guess I'm in the upper 49.

But you have come back to stay. And you took my little brother. What the hell were you thinking?

What do I have to say now? When I'm at a loss for words, I fall back on the wisdom of Sly and the Family Stone: Boom-shacka-lacka.

What do I have to say now? The words in this book.

Don't Fail Me Now

The problem, like most problems in life, probably had to do with his footwork.

~ Chad Harbach, *The Art of Fielding*

There, underfoot: a frog flattened on the driveway, splayed so thin you could scrape it up with a spatula. Only you wouldn't do that, because it's dead, and it used to be alive, it used to ribbit and hop. You step around it with care when your father walks you to the car, just as, soon, you will avoid every crack in the sidewalk, eyes scanning a few yards ahead as you fear for your mother's back.

Who made the step to the schoolbus so high? You don't want Kitty Reilly to witness the briefest of stumbles. It's a question of timing, making that last step look smooth. Why, in the hallway at school, can't anyone master the concept of single file? You establish a distance from the person ahead and you watch step by step, matching your pace to hers. In gym class, with the trampolette and the sawhorse, you have to hit the right stride for the take-off, one final leap and a reach for the pommels, a hip-swing left or right or the splits and then feet back together for landing. You hope Kitty's watching.

On the basketball court at recess, your body calculates the number of steps to the basket; for a right-handed layup you launch from your left foot, and vice versa. You learn that rebounding has more to do with position than with jumping: establish yourself between your man and the hoop, and he has no chance no matter how high he skies. And on defense, you hear the voice of Coach McKibben: move your feet move your feet MOVE YOUR FEET!

At dances, in the same gym, the same rules apply, but somehow you cannot apply them. There's Kitty Reilly across the way, dancing with her girlfriends, so cool and so lithe, and here are you, in a little clutch of hamstrung guys, head bobbing to the beat, arms crossed on your sunken chest, your proud new Adidas immersed in fast-setting cement. You gaze across the unbreachable distance like a Bedouin at a mirage. A mirage it may not be; it may be a real girl who would dance with you if only you would ask. Your feet will not take you there.

At home there's the dance with your father, when he makes a rare appearance at your bedroom, just to check in with his son. He stands outside the open door, his large veiny hand on the knob, ready to be invited in if his son wants to make such a gesture. You stand at the desk where you were writing. Your feet, in the slippers he paid for, already too small, don't know what to do.

Once he has turned back to the hall, you sit and contemplate the steps that will lead out of this house, this suburb, into a different life. It's the dance you've been rehearsing for years, and you will take it wrongfooted again and again.

And now, with fallen arches and clotted ankles, with wincing tendons and soles grown soft from too many years in dark socks and unsensible shoes, you just want to put your feet up, take a load off, rest your dogs. But still there are steps to be taken. No foot is the wrong foot.

THE SNOW MAN SPEAKS

In an exclusive *Snow Life* interview, his first in over thirty years, the celebrated snow sculptor George Putnam speaks out on the state of contemporary snow art, The Beatles, and the dramatic events of 1976.

Editor's Note: George Putnam, also known as "The Snow Man," is famously protective of his personal life. He has not participated in a public competition since 2007, and has not spoken to the press in decades. So the blogosphere was abuzz last month when he registered for the International Snow Sculpting Festival in Lake Geneva, Wisconsin, site of his earliest triumph. In an unsolicited e-mail, Putnam made it known to *Snow Life* that he was available for an interview. Our writer, Finis Porter, was already on the scene to cover the festival.

[Photo caption: Putnam and Sigridsdottir in 1972.]

The facts of George Putnam's life are quickly told. He

was born in 1931 in suburban Philadelphia, where his father sold life insurance. His mother was an unassuming homemaker; she died when her only child was eight. Young George was sent off to a New Hampshire boarding school, where he did not distinguish himself. He once summarized his time there as "twelve years reading all the books that no teacher assigned." In his art classes, he dabbled in the usual drawing and clay, but made no special impression on his instructors, one of whom later recalled him as "a silent and unyielding boy."

The recipient of numerous honorary degrees, Putnam did not attend college. At the age of twenty, he was working part-time in a Philadelphia bookstore when he happened upon the crucial turning point of his life—Beauregard's biography of Frederick Forster, the father of modern snow sculpture. "It was December," he later told a reporter. "The sky opened, and it poured down snow on snow."

For almost twenty years Putnam toiled unknown, traveling the north, learning his trade. He worked with various groups, but did not come to public notice until the International Festival of 1972, when he exhibited the first of his notorious "Dogs in Heat," popularly known as "Shnow Shtupping." That piece served notice to the staid world of snow sculpture: here was a talent to watch. It was at that festival that he met the Icelandic sculptor Sigrid Sigridsdottir, ten years his junior and already known for both her exquisite craft and her pale beauty. Their meeting, he later claimed, "melted the tundra for miles around." Then came the quicksilver years of their collaboration, which was always fraught with tension. Often they seemed to be at each other's throats, but again and again they shocked the art world with works like "The Loxodrome," "Helix the Cat," and "The Mystery Dance" — images that have since become part of the world's visual vocabulary.

Meanwhile, their private lives became fodder for the tabloids. In 1973 Sigridsdottir's marriage to New York financier Carl Levinson dissolved in acrimony. Putnam and Sigridsdottir moved from triumph to triumph until early in 1976, when their split was well documented by the popular press.

After Sigridsdottir's mysterious death later that year, Putnam disappeared from public view, remaining secluded at his home in western Maine. In 1984 he re-emerged at the International Festival with "Orpheus Ascending" — a single pyramid so severe, so sheer, some critics felt sure it was intended as a joke. The shape was ever so slightly skewed, its classical purity just a little off-center — "enough," said the critic Max Vorbeling, "for the viewer to sense that something was wrong, though no one could say what it was."

In subsequent years Putnam made only sporadic public appearances, but he still surfaced with several important sculptures, most notably his provocations on environmental themes like "Snow Leopard" (2002) and "Shambogoffin" (2007), that fabulous creature with the head of an osprey and the body of a double boiler. Those pieces brought a new following of politically engaged admirers, although some critics openly pined for the bad old days of "Dogs in Heat." Putnam's proposal for this year's International Festival was entitled "Baby Come Back" — apparently in homage to an obscure Philadelphia doo-wop band of the 1950s called The Paladins.

When word came last month that the legendary Snow Man was ready for an interview, we were naturally eager for a meeting. As it turned out, we never met in person. True to his reputation for perfectionism, Putnam insisted that the interview be conducted entirely by e-mail, and that it be printed exactly as written. He arranged for two extended sessions, two days apart, so that there could be an authentic back-and-forth in real time and also a chance for reflection between "meetings." Perhaps this was meant to approximate the real-time element of snow sculpting; there was a definite feeling of performance about it all. After posing each question, we were prepared for a pause, but the responses came quickly, in writing that was remarkably error-free. What follows is an unaltered transcript of the e-mails, which took place just before the opening of this year's festival .

Snow Life: Thank you for this opportunity. To begin: this is your first interview in over thirty years. Why now?

George Putnam: To everything there is a season.

SL: You haven't taken part in a competition since 2007.

GP: Is that a question?

SL: Well, why not?

GP: I'm 81 years old. I've had surgery to repair both knees and both shoulders, as well as a hip replacement; I have to be wheeled onto the sculpting space, and I work in a special harness that keeps me upright. My hearing isn't what it used to be. Competitions are enlivening—and they also knock me out.

SL: Some have suggested that this festival could be a kind of farewell.

GP: You never know. Actually, I'm feeling pretty good this morning. I dressed myself and ate my prunes and successfully moved my bowels. But the night comes when no man can work.

SL: Do you ever wonder what your life would have been like if you had been born in, say, Honduras?

GP: What the hell kind of question is that? I can't imagine living in Honduras, with all that fast water. I like my water slow.

SL: The past few winters have been the warmest on record, with increasingly smaller amounts of snowfall. Some analysts foresee the end of snow-sculpting as we know it.

GP: Aren't you the cheerful one. But yes, since you mention it, we're really and truly screwed. I heard on the radio this morning that the wood frogs are already emerging here in southern Wisconsin, and it's only February. Maybe we should be more concerned about the polar bears than about a few people who make things out of snow.

SL: You've won every prize in the world of snow sculpting. Your great contemporary, Sigrid Sigridsdottir, passed away long ago. Almost all of your competitors are in their thirties and forties. What keeps you going?

GP: I have already mentioned the prunes.

SL: Seriously.

GP: Seriously. I feel bad for my competitors, as you call them. They show up with their cell phones and their i-Thingies; they always seem to be looking at or talking into a little hunk of plastic; it's like they're not even there. The great thing about snow sculpting is that it's so elemental: no power equipment, no man-made components, just hand tools and H_2O and zero degrees centigrade. It's just sixty-five hours, from block of snow to finished sculpture. If they want to spend some of that precious time on their hand-held devices, good luck to them. My idea of a hand-held device is an eight-inch auger.

Sigrid did not "pass away." She died.

SL: Right. Maybe we can come back to that. But can you say more about your remarkable longevity? You first won the Frosty back in 1972, right here in Lake Geneva. Here we are forty years later, and word has it that you're working on something really astonishing. How do you do it?

GP: "The Frosty" is a vulgar term. It's the Frederick Forster Award for Frozen Sculpture.

SL: Sorry. The Forster, then.

GP: Yes, let's have a little respect for the pioneers. The field of snow sculpture would be nothing without Forster's groundbreaking work. When I first saw the pictures of his Xanadu, those caves of ice that gave an impression of limitless space, I could feel the hubris of Kubla Khan, I could practically hear the ancestral voices prophesying war. I knew then that we had to get out of Vietnam. And I started to feel the possibilities inherent in this great craft. To reduce its highest honor to a cartoon character is a desecration invented by some Madison Avenue shill in order to sell breakfast cereal. They are not grrrrreat. Forster was great.

How do I do it? I could tell you about transversal etching with a hand-cut riffler, but you don't really expect me to reveal trade secrets, do you? You want something uplifting about my work ethic or my religious faith or the inspiration of my father. Well, my father was a perfectly decent man who sold life insurance in Haddonfield, New Jersey and died of kidney poisoning. He rooted for the Phillies and he listened to Texaco at the Opera on the radio every Saturday, stretched out on our living room couch. He was deeply moved by the intermezzo of La Cavalleria Rusticana. That was the only time I saw him cry. I don't believe in insurance. I don't believe in inspiration. I believe in eight-inch augers.

SL: All right, then, let's talk about technique.

GP: That's like saying to a frog "Let's talk about insects." Technique is all there is.

SL: So you don't want to talk about details.

GP: Of course I can describe details. We're not really talking, by the way. We're typing. At a significant cost to my arthritic fingers. What do you want to know?

SL: Well, where do you get your ideas?

GP: That's not technique; that's the world just beyond the turn of your shoulder. You want me to tell you about opium dreams? Lucy in the Sky with Dihedrons? I get my ideas from my brain and my fingers and my as-yet-un-poisoned kidneys.

SL: Okay…Well, how do you get started? I mean, do you draw up a sketch? With a pencil, or with a computer? Do you conceive of a new piece in words first, or in images?

GP: Yes.

SL: Yes?

GP: All of the above. It depends on the sculpture.

SL: Well, with a sculpture like "The Loxodrome," for instance, one imagines that you drew pages of figures before committing anything to snow. As you probably know, Max Vorbeling has shown that it expresses the Golden Ratio perfectly. Did you think of that first? Or did that evolve as you worked on it?

GP: Max Vorbeling is the north end of a southbound horse.

SL: So the old feud is still alive?

GP: A feud requires two parties with relatively equal status. Montagues and Capulets. Hatfields and McCoys. In this case we have an artist and a not-artist who says patently foolish things about art. It's not a feud, it's an ambush. Max Vorbeling thinks a spherical sculpture with a fine tracery spiral etched in it has something to do with the Golden Ratio. He thinks this sphere expresses "the long pent-up desire of man for equilibrium in a world that is perilously out of balance." I'm quoting from *World of Snow*, that ponderous vehicle for the glorification of the sculpting critic. He's free to think what he likes, of course—but I'm also free to call him a jackass. Only that would be an insult to the donkey family.

SL: As a woman, I must say I wasn't crazy about that generic reference to the pent-up desire of "man."

GP: I wondered about the name Finis.

SL My grandmother's maiden name. Can we talk about this subject? There have been so few females in the field of snow sculpting. Why do you think that is?

GP: Usual reasons. Tradition. Assumptions that were hard to break down. When the great pioneers were getting started, back in the twenties, everyone just assumed that a woman's place was in the kitchen, not the meatlocker. That's where Forster got started, you know: he was working for a butcher, running into the meatlocker all day long for cuts of meat. This was back when refrigeration actually depended on blocks of ice that were delivered by the local ice man, cut from the nearest pond in winter and stored in a well-insulated cave or cellar. Those great crystalline slabs of ice, big enough to use as a couch, scored with the teeth of saws and punctured by the massive tongs that pulled them from the ice truck—those were the first great sculptures of the modern age. Even as a teenager in a butcher's smock, Forster saw the splendid forms they could take. How could Michelangelo look at a block of marble and see the shape of an angel in it? It was something in the veins of the stone, the contours of the surface grain; he could feel where it was more pliant to the touch. It was the same with Forster, after all that time in the meatlocker. And there weren't any women hanging out in meatlockers at the time. Sculpting just wasn't the sort of thing a woman did. It's hard physical labor, you know. Not that a woman can't do it, I'm not saying that. But people seemed to assume they couldn't.

SL: Until Sigrid Sigridsdottir.

GP: Until Sigrid. But of course she grew up in the ice fields of Keflavik, near the caves of Ronso; she was surrounded by glorious sculpture from birth. She didn't need a meatlocker for inspiration.

SL: Are you suggesting that she had it easier?

GP: Well, didn't she? How many great surfers come from Kansas?

SL: But she was a woman at a time when women weren't expected to go into such a masculine field. And yet she became the other great snow sculptor of her generation—your generation. In the news stories it was always "The Snow Man and the Ice Queen"; it was like Magic and Bird, or Fischer and Spassky. At first, they said you hated each other. And your styles were so different. You were the tough American, sounding your barbaric yawp in massive molten chunks; she was the craftsperson in the European tradition of filigree, as if lace curtains could be fashioned from snow.

GP: I always hated that "Ice Queen" stuff. That was purely for the tabloids.

SL: And yet they said that the two of you made each other better.

GP: We did.

SL: Can you say more?

GP: Sigrid…well, I did hate her, at first. She was just so… smug, with her "I'm from Iceland, what do *you* know about snow?" And she was so damn good. I mean, I thought it was just facile, you know, she grew up carving icicles in July, she could do a totem of all the heroes from the Eddas in her sleep. I thought, that's not art, that's just a native pastime, to impress the tourists. But then I saw pictures of her "Ugly Duckling" in *Snow Life,* and even though there was a lot of media hype about it, you know — "First Great Female Snow Sculptor Makes a Statement in a Man's World," blah blah blah, and there were some schlocky effects in it — too much willed pathos in the duckling, like "Look at me, I'm a poor widdle birdy, and did you notice that I'm female, too?" — still, even in those black and white photographs, that astonishing sequence in which the duckling somehow becomes the swan, all in one block of snow, and the swan is poised to take off on those masterful wings that make you believe it can fly — I could tell I was seeing genius. And now her work has been gone for almost forty years.

SL: But we have the photographs. We have that remarkable documentary, "Swan in Flight," in which the camera circles around the pieces so that you can see them from every side and almost feel their depths. We have the descriptions written by those who viewed the pieces. Books have started coming out, documenting the whole career.

GP: Photographs are all well and good. Some of my best friends are photographers. But photographs are flat. Films are flat. And warm. "Flat and Warm," that's what they should have called that documentary. Descriptions — well, what's the saying? Writing about snow sculpture is like dancing about architecture.

SL: And then there was the fire.

GP: Yes.

SL: What did you think about that?

GP: What do you mean, what did I think?

SL: Well, there were so many theories.

GP: There weren't so many. Either it was a terrible accident or it was part of a grand scheme, a kind of performance art. Ice Queen Goes Up In Flames. The headline writers feasted on the irony. Some say the world will end in fire: everybody quoted that. They loved the fact that the poet's name was Frost. It was almost as bad as being sponsored by a breakfast cereal.

SL: Some people thought you were involved.

GP: Did they.

SL: Well, you had recently broken up. The pictures were in all the magazines.

GP: That's enough for now. My fingers hurt.

The first installment of our conversation ended here. We resumed it two days later.

SL: Let's talk more about your practice. As everyone knows, snow-sculpting competitions usually involve teams of up to five members, because the physical work is too much for one person to complete within the time constraints. And yet you have largely been a solo artist.

GP: Forster used to do it all himself.

SL: But that was before all the advances of modern snow sculpting. Now it would be impossible for a single person to do everything—manage the block of snow, shovel or dig away the large sections that will become empty space, erect the scaffolding for work on the higher sections, carve the finer details, and so on.

GP: That's right, everyone works in gangs now. Team Vermont. L'Equipe Québecoise. The Winter Weasels. Those guys are good. But a lot of them are in it more for the beer than the sculpting.

SL: Sigridsdottir was essentially a solo artist, too. And yet you did such astonishing things together. How did that happen?

GP: I wish I knew. Some kind of alchemy. There's a poem in which Browning describes a musician who, out of two notes, made not a third note but a star. If I knew how it happened, maybe I could reproduce it. But if I reproduced it, that would be a copy, not the thing itself. I can only get up every day and do what is given me.

SL: By?

GP: What do you mean?

SL: "Given" implies a giver.

GP: I don't know. The universe. My father's failed career.

My mother's love. The oxygen provided by plants. The pizzicato opening of The Paladins' "Don't Forget Me."

SL: After Sigrid's death, you virtually disappeared, making only occasional appearances. Critics said you knew how to manipulate the public's interest, emerging just often enough to pique it. What were you doing?

GP: I drank a lot. I made some sculptures in the fields around my house. Some days I thought it was my best work ever—and the next day it struck me as utter nonsense. I emerged, as you put it, when I needed money. They were always willing to pay The Snow Man for an appearance. Even if I produced a lump of yellow snow, some idiot would acclaim my daring excremental vision. I'm not proud of that time. I wallowed in her absence.

SL: Why did you break up?

GP: Why did The Beatles break up? "Artistic differences."

SL: That's too easy.

GP: It wasn't easy at the time, I assure you.

SL: Tell us about it.

GP: Well, John fell in love with Yoko, and they started having all these wild ideas about sleep-ins and be-ins; and Paul wanted to get back to the old days of performing live the way they used to do in Hamburg, just four guys bashing out songs about holding somebody's hand…

SL: You know what I mean. You and Sigrid.

GP: I was only half-joking about The Beatles. Listen to "A Day in the Life." John opens with the spacey voice of over-whelmed fatigue, "I read the news today, oh boy," and Paul breaks in with the boppy energy of an ordinary day, "Woke up, fell out of bed, dragged a comb across my head ..." It's like Jekyll and Hyde both getting their licks, all in one five-minute blast of brilliance. No wonder it couldn't last. You can hear The Beatles' break-up all through that song.

SL: Like you and Sigrid in "Les Neiges d'Antan."

GP: More or less. A tug of war may be antagonistic — but the tension keeps the rope taut and both parties on their feet.

   After that, I just hired assistants who had no experi-ence. The ideal was a young man, strong enough to do the gruntwork, but without any training or even any brains. I could always find a few at the local liberal arts college. If they started showing an interest in the work, I let them go in a hurry.

SL: Sigrid said you used her that way, too.

GP: In that interview with Vorbeling.

SL: Yes.

GP: She wasn't in her right mind then. Vorbeling asked her all kinds of leading questions. She was hurt. She had a right to be. But that didn't make her an objective judge.

SL: She said you used her in your work.

GP: You couldn't work with someone so…brilliant, so — full of light — and not be influenced. Yes, my work gained in every way from knowing her. Does that mean I used her? Have you never used your husband in some way? You are married, right?

SL: Let's keep the focus on your work.

GP: If you want to talk about someone who used people, let's talk about Vorbeling. He used her to advance his career, just when she was at her most vulnerable. If he hadn't reopened all those wounds, and then sprinkled salt in them, she might still be here today.

An artist uses everything. It's what artists do. Do you think she didn't use me? Did you see her Waterfalls? Her Clouds? Of course you didn't; you weren't born yet. They were rough, of course, they were never finished — but that was my roughness. And she was welcome to it. Maybe she didn't know how to finish them. If she killed herself, maybe that's why. Not some schoolgirl's anguish over a breakup, but honest despair over a failure. She had gone as far as she could. There was only one way to go further.

SL: So you think it was suicide?

GP: I don't know.

SL: She was buried so quickly, no one could ascertain her condition at the time of the fire.

GP: Those were the wishes of her family.

SL: People said she was carrying your child. That year

she disappeared from view, when she was back in Iceland, refreshing herself. It came right after your breakup.

GP: She wanted to go home for a while. Did you ever go through a breakup?

SL: Some say she had already given birth.

GP: And Elvis is a great-grandpa, living in Montana. Why are you doing this hackwork?

SL: It's my job.

GP: It is not. You're a novelist. I read your book yesterday. And it's not bad. A little self-indulgent, a little purple in its prose sometimes, but not bad. You're an artist. Or you could be. So why did you sign up for this interview of The Great Man? Are you desperate for money?

SL: It happens that I've always admired The Great Man's work. I wanted to know if he's really the bastard they say he is. I wanted to ask him some questions of my own.

GP: Like what?

SL: Why did you break up?

GP: You're not going to let it go, are you?

She walked away.

SL: When?

GP: We were in my car. That old blue Ford shitbucket I loved so much. We were just driving aimlessly across the snowy fields of western Maine. It was one of those winter days when you can't see the sun, but the sky is blandly bright; everything looked off-white. I think I knew that our relationship was already over; we had stopped working together; we hardly talked anymore. But I had this idea that if we kept moving, if I kept driving and the car didn't run out of gas, it couldn't end. She had one of those damn Gauloises in her left hand, filling up the ashtray, and her right was clutching the grip above the passenger side window; she always did that, even when we were going 25 through a school zone.

We came into this little town, I don't know the name. We hadn't said anything for a long time. We stopped at a light. There was a bus station, with a bus for Boston idling at the curb. She got out of the car, just like that, and walked across the street to the bus. She stood at the door for a minute, because someone else was getting on.

And I just watched. I watched. The light turned green, and someone behind me honked. I pulled off the road, to the side opposite the bus, and I watched. Did she want me to get out and follow her? Did she want me to cry out Stop? Was she glad to wash her hands of me? I thought it was just this crazy-ass dramatic thing; she'd get over it, and we'd be back together.

Was she carrying my child? I don't know. If she was, what power did I have over that? It wasn't in my body. She got on the bus, and she paid for a ticket. She didn't have a suitcase or anything—her stuff was at my house a hundred miles away—but she had friends in Boston. She took a seat on my side of the bus, and she looked down at me from that window with the deadest look I ever saw. The bus wheezed, and pulled away.

SL: Do you wish now that the two of you had children?

GP: The sculptures are my children.

SL: But snow sculptures don't last!

GP: Thanks for the news bulletin.

And *your* children? When was the last time they called?

SL: This isn't about me.

GP: No? What would you say it's about?

SL: It's about you. And snow-sculpting. And the latest international festival.

GP: And yet you keep asking about Sigrid.

SL: That's part of what people want to know. Why does the Snow Man go on and on, while the Ice Queen died too soon?

GP: Maybe she died just in time.

SL: What do you mean?

GP: She had already done her best work. Her reputation, of course, would only grow. She was still young and beautiful. Now she'll never get older. Don't tell me you don't think about it. I've seen your dust-jacket photograph.

SL: Let's talk about this year's festival.

GP: What do you want to know?

SL: Well, the press release says your piece will be called "Baby Come Back," based on a song by The Paladins.

GP: Yes. Remember The Paladins?

SL: They were before my time.

GP: I know, dear—but they did make recordings. You know, for the gramophone? You can listen to their songs over and over on YouTube. That publicity photo of the band isn't exactly kinetic, but if you stare at it long enough, it takes on a certain poignancy.

SL: What do you know about my children?

GP: They were born in hope and raised in fear. They were a shot at something. Maybe it will still work out.

SL: You're a bitter old man.

GP: Wait until you're eighty-one. Someday soon the doorbell will ring, and I'll go to look through the peephole, and I'll see The Old Dude himself out there, sickle over his shoulder, peering out from under his hood with that permanent, elegant grin.

If you're lucky, Finis, you get thirty thousand days. Days like this one, with sunlight and prunes and a decent bowel movement. There aren't enough of them to spend regretting your losses.

But we do it anyway, don't we. What became of Forster? What became of Sigrid? Where are the long frozen winters of my youth?

I hope your children get in touch.

George Putnam did not complete a piece for the Lake Geneva festival. Or if he did, it was a Snow Man stunt. The spot on the platform devoted to "Baby Come Back" remained empty, except for a dust of snow. Some said this was the result of a flurry the night before; some said it was the sculpture itself. Putnam did not appear. All around, young sculptors were busy at their work.

[Photo caption: The empty pavilion at Lake Geneva.]

Finis Porter is the author of a novel, *The Wife's Lament*. She no longer works for this magazine.

BOSCOSCURO FLEURDUMAL

She wakes to the first birds thirling, freeping, misk-
ing among the sycamores. All night it was so warm,
the windows stand wide and the rising day smells of
fresh doughnuts. Down at the corner, the Koffee Kup is
making ready for the long-haulers. If they had air conditioning, like at Chlöe's house, she'd miss all this. There's
no sun yet, just a faintness around the window frame.
But the phoebes know: they're saying Piper, Piper, it's
your day.

Eleven! Two sticks side by side, back to back, one and
one. She has been scritching them in her school notebook
for days, for weeks, forever. Now she's up, bare soles more
solid on the floorboards than the day before, when she was
only ten. She murks down the dark hall, one hand to the
painty wall; she doesn't stop to pee. Here's momanddad's
room, door open in the hope of a breeze on this sultry
night. But it's not night anymore; listen to the birds.

They're not going to like this.

"Mom! Dad!"

A groan from her mother's side of the big bed, some stirring from her father's. Dad sleeps on the side closest to the door, even at the Super Eight when they drive to see Mama and Papa. When Piper can't sleep, when she has the heebie-jeebies, this makes it easier to climb in with Dad and not wake Mom; Mom doesn't need to know. But today, her day, Piper wants them both.

"Wake up!"

Dad is the one who gets up. Mom has been sleeping late lately.

He's wearing the dorky peejays with the powder blue snowflakes, and his hair is sticking out on the side where he grows it longer for the partial comb-over. One of these days she's going to sneak up with scissors when he's napping on the sofa and put him out of her misery. In the little kitchen the overhead light makes the walls yellower; one of her vintage drawings gleams on the fridge, smoke curlicuing from the chimney. They have assumed their positions — she at the old kitchen table, swinging her feet, he at the open pantry, scratching his neck.

"So what do you want for brekkers, Pippin?"

She waits.

"Buttered thrrrips?" He rolls the r's. "Battered chips? Shuttered ships?"

"*Dad*-dy."

He throws her a look. "Shattered hips?"

"Gross!"

"All right, then," he sighs, "if you inshmist, it will just have to be ze spécialité de la maison," and he honks *honh-honh-*

-honh like Maurice Chevalier. "Lost Bread à la Dad-dee."

She applauds.

"Now, where is that bread?" He looks in the fridge, under the table, behind her ear. "Not here, not here, not here…Oh, zut alors, eet ees lost!" She rolls her eyes. He pulls a loaf from the breadbox and trophies it over his head. "Could this be it?"

She knows her lines. "C'est ça!"

"Ça!" he cries. "Now we're cooking."

"You invented Gormic? That is so cool!"

He is sitting at a bar, listening to a young linguist with blond streaks in her hair. The sunlight blasting off the lake is so dazzling that every time he looks out the window his headache intensifies. They should be out on the deck on a day like this, enjoying the breezes off the lake; but it's ridiculously hot out there, meltingly hot, as if Global Warming has arrived to stay and is making its case in upstate New York.

He nods and takes a sip of his Rueful Dude. All the microbreweries are using hiply ironic names now, so the drinkerati can poke fun at themselves when they order a Middlebrau or a Lady Haha. The beer list for this place did not include a Blue Ribbon or a High Life.

She shakes her streaky head in disbelief. "I love Gormic. It's so clear it's, like, transparent. It's like everything you want a language to be—no ambiguities, no confusing homonyms like 'there,' 'their,' and 'they're,' no stupid apostrophes that can totally, like, change your meaning if you just, like, put one in the wrong place. God, my high school English teacher gave me so much shit about stuff like that."

She laughs and sips her beer. This is the moment for him to agree, to tell his own rueful dude story about high school English. But this young woman with the streaky hair and the fan-girl gaze is roughly the age of Piper, whom he hasn't seen in years. And he—well, he's old enough to know better. His wife would have laughed and said, "Go for it. What have you got to lose?"

When did young people start using words like "shit" so casually, in conversation with someone they've just met? His headache is starting to have a headache. He can see it in his mind's eye—the eye that isn't squinting at the blinding glare off the lake. His headache has become a cartoon character, staggering on the dazzled dock, holding its head and moaning, "Oy, oy, oy." He nods, and takes another sip.

She doesn't need more encouragement. She says, "I remember when I first discovered Gormic in grad school. I had been reading about all these constructed languages, like Esperanto and Sinderin and Klingon, and they were all just so, like, bogus, you know? I mean, did you know that every week more people hear Dothraki than Basque, Inuit, Yiddish, and—I forget, two other languages combined?"

Welsh and Navajo. He knows. He has just come from the same talk at the conlangers conference in the Ithaca Middle School auditorium, which does not feature air conditioning. He doesn't interrupt. She is talking about her discovery of Gormic, his own creation, as if it was on a level with her first kiss, or her first period; who is he to interrupt? He likes watching her rich full lips shape words like "bogus."

Gormic is his other baby. The one that stayed.

It was just a joke at first, something he did in his spare time. Especially that hard hard time. Even the name was a joke. "Gormless" is British slang for "clueless," "feckless." Well, he'd create something gormful. Gormic. It was a positive made from a negative, like feeling gruntled or looking sheveled.

The girl goes on. "It's all based on the Sapir-Whorf Hypothesis, right? We read about that in my class on the Metaphysics of Language. This is so cool. Language, like, limits consciousness, because we can, like, conceive of things only in terms of the words we have for them, which are, like, *riddled* with inconsistencies and nuances that depend on stuff like context and regional differences and even, like, facial expressions."

She lifts her fine-lined eyebrows at him. "I use the word 'like' a lot, don't I?" They both laugh. "I know, I know! It drives me crazy, too! But I can't help it. We studied this, too. It's a perfect example of the problems of 'natural' language. We're always, like, searching for the right words because language is so full of imperfections and ambiguities. I mean, look at English! Why do we pronounce 'slaughter' and 'laughter' so differently? How can a word like 'scat' mean 'scram!' and also 'animal feces' and also 'a form of jazz singing'? It's, like, insane! 'Like' is just our way of showing how, like, approximate everything is."

He nods. "Time flies like an arrow," he says, "but fruit flies like a banana."

She cracks up, dimples creasing her cheeks. "Exactly! It's all so freaking confusing! If a pitcher pitches and a catcher catches, why don't we say that a beaker beaks? A leper leps?"

They laugh at their own shared nerdliness; there is no greater pleasure. The cartoon of his headache has stopped holding its head. He says, "But a pitcher *doesn't* always pitch, because we use the same word for a container of liquid, and it doesn't pitch at all. But a sea pitches, and a battle can be pitched, or a tent, and the night can be as black as pitch…"

"I know, right? Where does it all stop? How do non-native speakers ever learn the damn language?"

"But it's not just English," he says. "It's any 'natural' language, all the languages since Babel."

"And that's why Gormic is so beautiful," she says, clinking her bottle to his. "It's so clear and logical and consistent. Thinking is hard enough already, right? They say we only use, like, ten percent of our brains. If we just had a language that made *sense*, with a totally consistent basis of word-formation and grammar, we could be more fully conscious, a hundred percent conscious!"

The sun has tilted slightly west; the lake is a platinum sheet. "Do you know," he says, "what my daughter's favorite word was, when she was a kid?"

She shakes her head.

"'Preposterous.' I know, it's a big word for a kid, but she was like that. I told her what a crazy word it is, how it means 'before' and 'after' all at once, both 'pre' and 'post,' you know, ass over teakettle, all out of kilter. She loved that."

"That is so sick!" the girl says.

He pauses.

"I mean that in the good way," she adds, and they laugh. "So you have a daughter?"

He signals to the barman by pointing to their beers and raising two fingers. Now there's a universal language.

After breakfast, they take Biscuit for a walk, leaving Piper's mother to rest at home. She rests a lot these days. On the way to the park they pick up Chlöe, the BFF; Dad calls her Umlaut. Chlöe wears jeans and stripey t-shirts, and she's a monster on the monkey bars. Piper is already in her yellow birthday dress with the frilly bow beneath her nonexistent bosom, but she goes for the knee-swing move anyway, because it makes the blood rush to her head and the world go upside down, and who cares if her panties show? Who says eleven is too old for the monkey bars? Chlöe can hang there forever. But she, Piper, doesn't need to prove anything, and besides, the backs of her knees have started to burn.

"What do you call this, Dad?" She points to the pinkly chafed skin behind her knee.

"I call it the dorst."

"No, really."

"Really. You asked me what I call it. The dorst! Umlaut, tell your friend: do I lie?"

"Your dad does not lie, Pipe. He may be a weirdo, but he does not lie."

He bows. Chlöe bows. Piper shouts, "Time for Buns & Noodle!"

Her father used to have a job. He still does, technically, but he is on "indefinite leave." She heard her parents talking about how they could afford this hiatus, or couldn't afford it; it was complicated. She was sitting at the top of the stairs, out of sight but still within earshot of their big chairs in the living room. The voices got low; the pauses grew.

At the bookstore, she and Chlöe race up the escalator as if it wasn't moving, intent on the section her father calls "Yah." As in, "No more of that Yah nonsense! When are you going to read some *books*?"

"These *are* books!" She leafs through one, under his nose. "Look: Words! Pages! People! The End!" She knows that he actually loves her reading habit; she thinks he even loves her Young Adult books. Why else was he so crestfallen when she said she didn't need him to read to her anymore? "Crestfallen" is a Daddy word. Anyway, this is her day: she's allowed as many *Pretty Little Liars* as she wants. Chlöe points a finger at her own mouth and gags. Chlöe is more of a *Wimpy Kid* kid. They grab books, sack out back to back on a beanbag chair, and disappear. He gets to browse for thirty minutes. Bliss.

Doctor 1 said, "There's an 80 per cent chance you're cured."

"Cured?" She hadn't expected that word.

"Yes." He was brisk and busy, thick dark hair bristling above his brows. He smiled. "I'd take four to one odds anytime."

She saw her doubtful face in the reflection of his glasses, twice, bright in the fluorescent light of the examining room. Was she really that pale? Piper sometimes razzed her about looking like a zombie. She had never been a player of odds. Maybe this summer she would devote herself to getting that tan.

"Of course, we'll monitor your progress with an x-ray every three months and a CT scan once a year. You never know."

"Of course." She thought the doctor was disappointed: he had delivered his big news, and she hadn't even cracked a smile. She wanted to keep her cool, the way her husband would. Mister Moderation. She was already rehearsing what she'd say to him in the waiting room.

"Cured, honey! Like a ham!" She wanted to be like Oscar Wilde. On his deathbed, he took exception to the wallpaper. "One of us has got to go," he said. If it wasn't true, it should be.

"Four to one odds!" she'd say to her husband. "That's the line in Vegas."

First, though, she had to get out of this ridiculous hospital johnny. She'd work on that flabby ass this summer, too.

Doctor 2 said, "This does not happen often. But it does happen."

Doctor 2 had wiry hennaed hair that corkscrewed above her dark-framed glasses and almost hid her dangly ceramic earrings. She spoke with a slight middle-European accent, as if she had learned in primary school never to use contractions and she was not going to start now.

She said, "We will map the best course of treatment for your specific condition. You will work with the nurse to maintain your weight and get enough protein. You must get a lot of protein. The radiation is calculated to kill only the bad cells, but there is always collateral damage. Your body will be working hard to regenerate itself, and for that it needs protein. I understand you are vegetarian?"

She nodded. Ever since she read that book about the industrial food system. If slaughterhouses had glass walls, we'd all be vegetarians. "Collateral damage" made it sound like she was a Vietnamese village in 1968. She watched her reflection nod, twice, in the doctor's stylish glasses. It had been three years since Doctor 1, and she still looked just as pale. When she put on a swimsuit, Piper said, "Behold: the Undead!"

"What will you do for protein? Beans? Nuts?" Doctor 2 sounded like an Old Country grandmother. Who would eat beans if they could have beef?

This, too, made her think of Piper. For a while, her daughter had gone along with "the veggie thing." She had said to her beloved Biscuit, "Those hamburger-munchers would probably eat you, too!" But then she became a teenager, and all bets were off. Her face stretched out, she got her ears pierced, and she went with her friends to Chick-Fil-A. What could her mother say? Her father, Mister Sweet Reason, said she had to make her own decisions. Biscuit died at a ripe old age. Piper and Chlöe went their separate ways—Chlöe into theatre, Piper to the mall. Her mother wondered sometimes if the babies had been switched at birth. Mister Understanding said it was a phase. Piper said, "Seitan? Who eats that stuff?"

Doctor 2 said, "Perhaps during the treatment you could modify your diet?"

"Perhaps."

Doctor 2 waited.

"But I think I can get enough protein from other sources."

The lady doctor sighed. "We are going to do all this work to save your life, and you cannot make this little change? I ask you to think."

She said she would. Think. She saw herself reflected twice, pale and thin and thinking.

On the radiation table, every day for eight weeks, she thought of James Bond. The red beam came out of the ceiling in the gleaming steel-paneled room. "You expect me to talk, Goldfinger?"

"No, Mr. Bond. I expect you to *die*."

But everyone knew he wouldn't. Die. Because he was Bond. Because it was a movie. She would tell her husband about this when she got back to the waiting room; he'd appreciate the allusion. Maybe.

Doctor 3 lowered his head with a sad smile. He was a sturdy man whose hair had probably once been red. She saw the lights of the examination room gleaming off his ruddy head. She had asked if now, after the radiation, after the chemo, it was just a matter of time. The lowered head said it all.

"But," he said, raising his eyes again, "We can't know how much time. It could be years."

Talk about phases. There was an orange food phase: it was autumn, and everyone kept bringing her butternut squash soup and pumpkin bread. There was a milkshake phase, when she couldn't eat anything solid. There was a don't-want-to-eat-anything phase. Well, her ass started looking better. Piper was quieter and quieter, at home less and less. Mister Sensible said she was fine; she just needed some time to herself.

The nurses didn't talk about shit. When the medication provoked diarrhea, great chattering rains of excrement, they spoke of "loose stools." As if she were the barroom of the Titanic. They asked about her "movements," as if she were a jewel-encrusted clock. They tracked her "evacuations," as if she were a city under siege.

In the reflection of Doctor 3's wire-rimmed glasses, she

imagined herself straightening up and asking, "How many years? What kind of years?" Once for each reflection, with the voices a little out of sync, as if someone had turned on the reverb. How many? What kind? She didn't want to let him off the hook with his sad-smile-looking-down routine. Years? Could? That means it could also be months, right? Right? Her reflection howled, twice.

But she nodded and didn't say anything.

Of course the streaky-haired woman asks for a demonstration. Conlangers always want a demonstration. They have all seen his website and marveled at the twenty-two grammatical categories for verbs (English has six), the system of declensions, the network of nouns and pronouns mapped out like rhizomes beneath it all. No one actually speaks Gormic, or even reads it. It was never supposed to be spoken. As soon as people begin speaking a language, it starts to evolve, to accumulate idiosyncrasies, and ceases to be the perfect thing imagined by its creator. Gormic was just an effort to show that things don't have to be the way they are — that we don't have to accept "natural" language just because it's all we've ever known. He was astonished when his website started accumulating hits, and then the admiring comments. How did you do it? they want to know. I was in between jobs, he says. I had some time on my hands.

"Can you show me a passage?" she asks.

He unfolds a cocktail napkin on the bar, takes a Bic from

his pocket, and writes for a minute. He knows that she is watching, rapt. This moment always amuses him. He is the gnomon around which all shadows fall. He could scribble anything—a right-wing rant, a sales pitch for snuff, the purest gibberish. How would she know?

"There," he says, and slides the napkin to her on the bar.

She studies it briefly. His penmanship has always been meticulous. "What does it say?"

He points at the words as he speaks them. "Boscoscuro fleurdumal," he says. "Finzicontini scheherazader mingelfarben." He catches himself and puts in a crutsicrig over the g.

"Cool!" she says. "What does it mean?"

"Mean?" he says. "You want it to mean?"

They pick up party supplies before leaving Buns & Noodle. Piper wants a Nook for every gift bag. Her father says how about each girl gets one of those individually wrapped almond cookies instead? Class-ee. They compromise on little notepads with matching detachable pens. Piper and Chlöe choose a different Yah novel for every bag. "Who gets *Witch & Wizard*?" asks Chlöe.

"Luck of the draw," says Piper.

They have lunch at Sugar 'n' Spice, Piper's fave, and carry out a hummus wrap for Mom, who won't eat it. But anyway.

Then it's time for swimming. "Swimming" means

changing into bathing suits and going out to the back yard where the plastic wading pool is. They don't want to swim, anyway. They clear away pine cones and lay out beach towels, then settle in for some serious gab. Is Rob Miller cute, or what? But when will he ditch those tassel loafers? For reals. Dad doesn't let them lie in the sun, but they move their towels as soon as he goes in to check on Mom.

They fought. They faught. They faut. They fot.

Most of the fights were over Piper — or at least it seemed that way at the time. She said he was too lenient, he said she was too strict. She said a child needs limits, he said a child needs to breathe. She told Piper they expected her to take care of them when they were old and feeble; she was only half-joking. He said, "Make your own life, Pippin." She said he just wanted to be Mister Nice Guy; he said she would have made a good Nazi. He said he didn't mean it.

She said morulating pegamoid, he said farfalloni metroland. She slept a lot. He invented Gormic.

When she was sickest, Piper went to stay at Chlöe's.

Near the end, she stopped sleeping. She wanted to taste all the lasts. The last cup of coffee, the last glass of wine, the last sunrise. She said he should move on. He said blank shrug.

Piper was out when she vamooshed.

*

The party goes well. Everyone admires her dress. Tina Woodward gives her the coolest set of interlocking brace-lets, just like the ones Tina's sister wears. They all seem to like their gift bags. Missy Favreau gets the *Witch & Wizard*. Dad is at his Daddyest, master of the revels, serving up cake with panache. "Would you like some panache with that?" He ashes his invisible cigar.

The cool thing about a June birthday is how long it lasts. When Mr. Woodward arrives to pick Tina up at 8:00, it's still broad daylight. Piper invites him in, ushers him through the house into the back yard, persuades him to put on a party hat, sit on a picnic table bench, take off his socks and shoes, and dangle his feet in the wading pool. Who could say no to the eleven-year-old in the yellow party dress, with a smear of white frosting on her cheek?

The sun is fading; the heat of the day has broken; the trees are full of swifts and swallows, preparing to carry the evening aloft. Even the grown-ups don't want to go in yet. The air tastes like meringue. A girl in a green pin-afore reels down the slope away from the house, arms outstretched.

After his wife died, he made lunches. He stood in the yellow kitchen early, while his daughter slept, and con-structed sandwiches. Piper wouldn't eat the whole-grain bread; she said ptui. She said pitooey. She wanted the kind of bread that melts in your mouth, the kind they

chop into little cubes for communion. He spread mayon-
naise while not listening to the news on NPR, the latest
disasters and depredations, nickering in the NASDAQ,
fluttering of the FTSE. He laid on lunch meat and a cheese
single, two crinkle-cut rounds of pickle, and lowered the
bookend slice of bread like a lid. Sealed it in a baggie, a
double handful of corn chips in another. Nestled them in
a paper bag, with an apple or a pear; Piper didn't go for
grapes. Two oatmeal raisin cookies. Set it on the counter
by the door.

The streaky-haired woman has stood up from her bar-
stool. She wants to go back to the conference. "There's
a talk debunking Tolkien tonight! That old bugger has
been, like, Lord of the — you know, Things — for too long.
They say his runes are, like, totally inauthentic. Are you
coming?" She pats her hip. Is this a gesture of invitation
in Young Personese?

He shakes his head. The sun may have scrammed,
but he knows it's still hot as boiling pitch out there. He
doesn't want to hear someone debunk Tolkien. He thinks
Tolkien should be bunked. He wants to nurse another
Rueful Dude. He is in kilter right here. He raises a bottle
to the backside of the girl as she goes. Nice dorst.

After everyone has left — Chlöe is the last to go — he lets
Piper stay up as late as she wants. It's her day. She's

never going to bed. She puts one of his records on the old turntable in the living room, and blows the invisible dust from the needle. Wild thing, dah-dah-dah-dah-dah, you make my heart sing. She spins her new bracelets and twirls. She curls on the couch to read *Pretty Little Liars*, and falls asleep in seconds. He carries her up to her sleeping mother's side. Biscuit climbs in, where Biscuit is not allowed. He puts on his dorky peejays and lies down, too. The future will unfurl, but not today. Not today. Words, pages, people, the end.

What Would I Have to Give You?

There once was a beanheaded boy with a bright colored stick in his hand. He was bad bored. The walls of the world were so white you couldn't even see they were walls. There was no one around. Nothing to do. Where was everyone?

He stretched, and the stick made a purple mark on the white something behind him. Not behind him, really, but around him, somehow, in every direction, just at arm's length. The mark zigzagged toward the top of the room he wasn't in: it had no ceiling or floor. The mark made a line from here to Glocca Morra. Here was the end of his hand.

He stretched again, and again. More lines, veering above and about and below. The beanheaded boy decided to go for a walk.

Where were his parents? Where were his pants? Who would remember to get the oil changed in the car? What car?

Outside, it's present tense, and it's brighter than bright. It's not even outside, really: there is no in. With the bright colored stick he makes a moon, almost half full, and you can't tell that in the unfull part there's really more moon. There might as well not be. Maybe there's not. It looms on the sky above him. Moon looms. This is good. Walk on, little beanhead.

Beanhead makes a road, straight as a beam, all the way to the horizon. He beams. Now he's got somewhere to go.

But it's not as easy as it seems, this walking somewhere. The road is too straight, bad boredom lurks, and the horizon stays out too far. He takes a shortcut across a field.

How can he take a shortcut when he has no destination? Oh, it's not that there's no destination; it's just that he doesn't know what it is. The shortcut will lead him there, though it may take a week and a day. And a wheelbarrow. It could be anywhere in eastern Cincinnati. Stones will bristle in the road. Dogs will shout in derelict yards. Burs will cling to his footy peejays. Moon will loom. Beanhead walks on.

In a basement bedroom, three fifteen-year-old guys are working on a project for school. It's a white house on a bluff in the woods, just off Clock Hill Road. The basement is dark, but just partly: on the back side, where the bluff recedes, it's above ground, with a window and a door to the back yard and a little scoop of gravel for cars. It's not a yard, really — just a brief clearing that holds back the woods behind the house. There's room in the gravel for two cars, but only one Buick waits there now.

In the basement bedroom, Asher sits crosslegged on the smooth cement floor, which is covered with a threadbare old carpet. He is intent on a magazine, scissors poised. A light bulb dangles in a conical metal shade above him, throwing glints off his tight dark curls. Across the room, Danny puts a record on the turntable, sets it in motion, and drops the stylus. He shakes the thick brown hair from his eyes and waits. The record pops and hisses.

They're making a photo-montage movie, one image at a time. First they pore over recent magazines, black and white images of the war, ghettos burning, sunsets over oceans they've never seen. It's just the old magazines Asher's parents get, nothing remarkable, *Life*, *Time*, *Look*, but everything's remarkable now — the war, ghettos burning, a basement bedroom, "Bringing It All Back Home" on the stereo. The boys cut photos from the magazines and lay them on a black cloth beneath the camera, perched on a tripod. By turns they get up and lean over the viewfinder, to confirm the choice of image and the framing. It's Asher's camera, but he wants them all to have a say. How much light for the shot of the White House that will be followed by the tenement in flames? How long to sustain that irony? What will Mr. Van Arsdale say?

"Oh, Van Arsdale's cool," says Danny. "As far as he's concerned, we could throw in that shot of Barbarella too."

"No, no," Beanhead says, "that would ruin the tone!"

"Okay, jeez, I was only joking. I'll do the X-rated version on my own."

The camera whirrs. Asher holds the aperture open long

enough to offer just a glimpse of the White House before it morphs into a smoking ruin. Juxtaposition is every-thing.

Beanhead loves being here in a basement bedroom, laughing with these guys. He has known them since grade school, but for a couple of years he has been busy with other things—Student Council, the baseball team, Pep Squad. Things that will be good for the college appli-cations. His sister and brother did these things, and they got into good colleges. And he doesn't hate doing them: he's a good shortstop, and somebody has to be in Stu-dent Council, right? Except that he does hate it, too. He doesn't know exactly what Asher and Danny have been doing while he has been burnishing his résumé—but he wants to know. The war keeps getting worse. At the breakfast table, his father's mouth tightens at the head-lines, but he doesn't say anything. On summer mornings, when Beanhead accompanies his mother to pick up their maid down in Madisonville, he sees the boarded-over storefronts, the black kids playing in broken glass. Life. Time. Look.

Now it's fall, and Mr. Van Arsdale has given them this assignment to create their own response to current events, using images or poetry or music. Danny says it's a rare chance to do something interesting at that bullshit school. They all live in the same leafy neighborhood, so it's easy to work together after classes. Asher has the camera and the basement bedroom where they can do the work. He and Beanhead have already made the soundtrack for the movie, using the little reel-to-reel tape recorder Beanhead got for his birthday. They propped the microphone on a chair in front of a big speaker in Beanhead's living room, then played carefully chosen snippets from albums on his father's big stereo. Dylan, Crosby Stills and Nash, Laura Nyro with the burning dark eyes. They took care to get it done in afternoons before Beanhead's father got home: he didn't care for those long-haired musicians. But Beanhead's mother always welcomed them; she encouraged her son to spend time with Asher, especially after the accident.

Beanhead doesn't know what happened, exactly. He never knew Baird Parks, who was eight years older than Asher and his twin sister Jessie. He just knows that one night back in the summer Baird's car slammed into an overpass on I-75, and he didn't survive. He was the only one in the car. Asher didn't talk about it. He immersed himself in their project, and Beanhead figures this is for the best.

The shortcut leads to a forest. He's afraid the forest will be dark, so he draws it with only one tree. How can it be a forest with only one tree? It's Beanhead's world; this is his forest. Moon looms above it.

The one tree sprouts apples. What if someone comes along to steal them? He makes a dragon that coils around the trunk—and the dragon scares him so bad that his hand, held out behind him, starts shaking. The bright colored stick, gripped tight in that hand, makes a wavy line. Backing away from the dragon, he falls in the waves. Moon beams on the water.

Every day after school, the three boys meet on the bus. Beanhead has to be home by six to clean up for dinner. He doesn't want to be there when his father gets home from work at five; that would mean conversation about how his day went, what he's doing in school. He isn't doing anything in school, just holding his hand up to answer dumb questions. In spring he'll have baseball practice. But this is fall, the world's best season. The boys get off the bus at Asher's stop, and scuffle through the leaves to the house up on the bluff.

In the kitchen, Asher's mother is smoking and listening to the radio. She is a gruff-voiced woman with glasses dangling from a cord over her chest; her long straight hair, streaked with silver, is pulled back in a ponytail. She greets them and offers to make sandwiches. Asher says no, they've got to work to do. She puts down her cigarette and gives him a look, then nods. No one smokes at Beanhead's house; his father quit when the Surgeon General's report came out. He says you'd have to be a moron to keep smoking now.

Asher leads the boys downstairs; his room is directly below the kitchen. As soon as they're down there, Danny says, "Hey, man, I wouldn't have minded a sandwich."

Asher says, "I'll get you something later, okay?"

They get to work. "Work" means riffling through old magazines and listening to Dylan and talking about Megan Prestwick's legs in those micro-miniskirts. Megan hangs out with Jessie sometimes; occasionally they get a glimpse of her here in the house on the bluff. Danny and Beanhead aren't even close to cool enough for Megan Prestwick, but Danny always perks up when he sees her car in the space behind the house. She's a year older and already driving. "Is she upstairs?" he asks with a grin. "I can feel the sexy from here!"

"Cool your jets, Moore," says Asher. "Megan is not upstairs. Jeez, you're just like our dog when he's chasing cars. If he caught one, he wouldn't know what to do with it." Danny smiles. "Just try me."

Asher swats him on the head with a magazine. "I'm going to keep the fire hose ready." Danny swats him back, and a slanging match begins. Beanhead is eager to push the work ahead: they have to finish the filming today, so it can be developed in time to present it in class next week. But what can he do? He knows when this is going to end: when "Subterranean Homesick Blues" begins. As soon as the band kicks in, Danny starts playing air guitar, and all three of them wail along: "Johnny's in the basement mixin' up the medicine, I'm on the pavement, thinkin' 'bout the government ..."

When the song is over, Danny says, "More music, maestro!" Asher looks for "Blonde on Blonde," and says, "Damn, it must be up in the living room. I bet Jessie was playing it there." Beanhead says, "I'll get it."

*

With one hand holding the bright colored stick above the water, he makes a trim little boat, and sets sail. Moon sails along with him. Soon, he makes land.

He notices that he's hungry, and he makes all kinds of pie. Ham, lamb, sheep, mutton, wild hog, and prairie dog. He can't eat them all, so he makes a skinny moose and a smiling porcupine: they scoff up the rest. And off he goes, looking for a hill to climb, to see where he is. He starts drawing a hill and climbing, moon above his eyes. If he goes high enough, he should be able to see the window of his bedroom.

Beanhead goes up through the kitchen, where Mrs. Parks is still at the table smoking, reading the *Post-Times Star.* That's what his father will be doing by now, minus the cigs, a mile away, in another dimension.

She looks up. "You want some lemonade, son?"

"No thanks, Mrs. Parks, I've just got to grab a record in the living room."

She nods and turns back to her paper.

When he reaches the front hall, Beanhead doesn't stop at the living room; instead, he turns up the stairs to the second floor. In a moment he's opening the door to a bedroom at the top of the stairs. He can say he thought the album might be up here.

The room is unnaturally neat: no one has slept here in

months. The windows are closed, but brilliant autumn sunlight dapples through. Beanhead goes over to one of them. Dangling from the ceiling in front of it is a mobile made of wire and string, with seashells and shards of colored glass glinting in the sun. On the wall are black-and-white pictures of Asher and Jessie as tow-headed kids tussling in a back yard somewhere. Then there's a picture of Baird, with a dark mustache, standing by a car.

"Help you find something, Beanie?"

And there is Jessie, leaning against the doorframe. She's wearing rust-colored hip-huggers and a peasant blouse; caramel hair falls over her shoulders and frames her sleepy hazel eyes. Her voice is soft and low. No one calls him that anymore.

"Um, no, I'm fine. I'm just looking for, for …"

She steps in, and looks at the wall. "That one is in Madeira, before we moved up here. I loved that little wading pool. I swear it's why I became a swimmer. I always wanted to be in the water." She laughs a husky laugh. "That one was Halloween. Asher dressed as a cowboy and wanted me to be the Indian, but I wanted to be a marlin. Mom didn't know how to make a marlin costume, so I just went in my bathing suit and flippers. I froze my little tushie off."

She seems to want to talk. He lets her continue.

"That's Baird just before he left for college. Funny, that's six years ago, but it's still the way I think of him now." She leans in close. "Can you see, if you took off the mustache, he'd look exactly like Asher?" She covers it up with a finger. "See what I mean? Ashie doesn't think so, but people can be blind when they want to be, you know?" Beanhead nods, and gets a whiff of wheat germ and honey shampoo.

"Asher blames Mom for pushing Baird away. He thinks it wasn't an accident."

"What do you think?"

She sighs, and looks at the wall again. "God, I don't know. I mean, yeah, it was ridiculous the things they fought over. First she wouldn't let him wear bellbottoms. Can you imagine? Then it was his hair. Then he brought a girlfriend home, and she caught them in this room." She looks at the bed, now made up neatly with a blue chintz spread, and shakes her head. "He should have known better, you know? Mom and Dad grew up in the South, in the thirties; you just didn't do that kind of thing in your parents' house. I think he did know better. I think he wanted to get caught, to put it all in her face."

Beanhead nods, and stays focused on the pictures. She goes on.

"And maybe he knew she would kick him out of the house, too—that's my theory. He wanted to leave, but he knew she wouldn't approve. Unless he forced her hand."

"But if it wasn't an accident, then...why?"

"Asher thinks he didn't feel loved enough." She looks Beanhead in the eye, inches away, then holds her small brown hands open, as if making ready to catch a ball. "But who does?"

She looks at the picture of Baird again. "I think she loved him as well as she knew how."

"What about your father?"

"Oh, Dad was always cool about it all. He thought Baird would find his own way. But he couldn't stop Mom from being Mom. I kind of admire her for that: she's a tough old bird. But Asher won't forgive her."

She looks at Beanhead, eyes wide. "Do you know what he does at night?"

He shakes his head.

"He wanders all over Clock Hill. I hear him coming and going sometimes; my room is right above the back door. He goes out into those woods, and sometimes he doesn't come back until four or five in the morning. I don't know how he gets up for school. I worry that he'll just fall into some abyss."

She gazes at the mobile dangling by the window. "What's the point of not forgiving?"

Then there's the sound of tires on gravel, and a car horn sounds in the driveway. "I gotta go," she says. "I hope you find what you're looking for." And she hurries down the stairs, shouting to her mother as she goes.

Beanhead backs out of the room and closes the door. Downstairs in the living room, he finds "Blonde on Blonde," the double LP with the cover photo of Dylan in a brown suede coat, out of focus, his lip in a skeptical curl. Beanhead's father wanted to know what the title meant, and Beanhead couldn't say. Did it mean two girls? When he played it on Dad's stereo — he didn't have his own yet, so he had to listen to stuff in the living room — his father winced at Dylan's smoky howl and said, "When is this fella going to die?"

On his way back through the kitchen, Mrs. Parks isn't sitting there anymore — just an ashtray full of butts, filters smeared with lipstick.

The hill becomes a mountain; the moon is partially obscured behind it. Little Beanhead keeps climbing, but the mountain starts to crumble beneath his feet, and he begins to fall, ass over teakettle, bright colored stick flailing in the empty air.

"What kept you?" asks Danny when he gets back downstairs. "A little quickie with Megan?"

"What do you mean?" Beanhead takes the record to the turntable. He doesn't know what a quickie is, but he knows it's dirty.

"Don't play innocent with us, Marsden. I saw her car pull up out back."

Beanhead stays focused on the stereo. He places the needle on the record and turns to Asher, hunched over the viewfinder. "What have you guys done without me?"

Asher looks up. "Don't worry, we didn't pull the trigger on anything. We've just been looking at that sequence on Mississippi." Thanks to Dylan songs like "Only a Pawn in Their Game," Asher knows all about Medgar Evers and

Emmett Till. He knows how polluted the mainstream is. He says the revolution is coming soon.

Right now, though, Danny is ticked off about the music for their film. "We're not really using that 'Homeward Bound' bit, are we? Simon and Garfunkel are pussies."

Asher sighs. "We've been through this, Danny. The music is set. We just have to time the images so they work with the rhythms and the words on the tape."

"Yeah, well, thanks for consulting me."

"Hey, don't blame us. You were messing around with Sheila Meadows at the time."

Danny smiles. "Ah, the lovely Sheila. But we can just do the tape over, now that we have a better idea of the images."

Beanhead breaks in. "But it's due next week! We don't have time to do it over! We have to finish it today!" He doesn't add that he's not allowed to use the stereo now, after his father came home from work one day and found they hadn't turned it off. He said you'd burn out the whole system that way.

Danny says, "Fine, stick with the stupid Simon and Garfunkel. La-la-la-la-la. Maybe we should throw in The Monkees while we're at it."

Then he smacks the back of the chair Asher's sitting in. "But what if we did something crazy with the images in that scene, like, I don't know, nothing but blackness?"

Beanhead says, "But that's not part of the plan! We've got it all laid out."

"Right. Like Nixon has a secret plan for peace. Sometimes

you just have to make it up as you go along, you know?"

"But how would a sudden black-out comment on the war?"

"Who says it has to comment?"

"But the assignment is about current events! If it doesn't comment, what is it?"

"It's art! Art doesn't have to comment. It just is. Warhol did a five-hour movie of a guy sleeping."

"Who would want to watch that?"

"That's not the point!"

"Isn't it? Shouldn't we care what people want to watch?"

"No! You're the artist, you decide! You teach them what they want. Anyway, who cares what they want? It's our film! Who are they?"

"They're our audience!"

"Oh, so you're going to make decisions based on what Rick Labombard wants? Rick Labombard wants his mommy!"

Beanhead looks at Asher, who has been sitting back and listening. "So? Asher? What do you think?"

"I think it's time for a sandwich," he says.

Little Beanhead draws a hot air balloon and a basket, and sails away from the crumbling mountain, moon on his shoulder. There's no sign of his bedroom window. How long can he fly?

*

In the kitchen, they make sandwiches—chipped beef, Kraft singles, and Miracle Whip on rye, with crinkled pickle slices. Asher and Danny decide to run outside and play Kill the Man in a big pile of leaves. Beanhead can't stand to leave the bread and cold cuts sitting on the counter, the plates unwashed. He puts the lid on the Miracle Whip. He sees by the kitchen clock that it's 5:30. He has to get home. But they have to finish the film.

Outside, the guys are lying in a pile of leaves, out of breath from laughing. Beanhead says, "Uh, guys? We have to get back to work."

Danny says, "Who made you king?" He grabs Beanhead by the ankle and pulls him off his feet into the leaves. "Okay, Marsden, what would I have to give you to make you punch your grandmother right in the face? A hundred dollars?"

This is a favorite game. Beanhead laughs. Then Danny says, "Really. What would I have to give you? A thousand?" His eyes are dark as acorns.

Beanhead says, "You don't have a thousand dollars."

"Of course I don't—but right now, when I'm asking this question, I do. Ten thousand dollars?"

"Danny, I'm not going to punch my grandmother in the face."

"Not for ten thousand dollars? Seriously? Think what you could do with ten thousand bucks. Think of that Martin guitar you want. Imagine the car you could buy." Then he hits below the belt. "You could go to any college

you want." Beanhead's father says he can't go to college
in the northeast, because those places are full of godless
liberals. Drugs, free love, sit-ins—New England colleges
have been all over the news. Beanhead has never been
north or east of Columbus, but New England is where he
longs to be.

"How hard would I have to hit her?"

"Hard. A real punch. But only once."

"Could I wear a disguise?"

"No disguises. Full knowledge is part of the deal."

"Do I get to tell her why I'm doing it? If I'm going to
get ten thousand bucks, Granma might be willing to take
a fall."

"No, you've got to cold-cock her, no explanations."

"Nope. Couldn't do it."

"Couldn't, or wouldn't?"

"Same difference."

"No, it's not. You mean wouldn't."

"Okay, wouldn't. I wouldn't do it."

"Fifty thousand?"

"What have you got against my grandmother?"

"Nothing. I'm sure she's a sweet old lady. What would
I have to give you?"

"What would I have to give you to go back in and finish
the movie?"

"You couldn't afford it."

"Asher?"

Asher has been lying still in the leaves, looking at the
sky. "He's right. The movie is a bust. It's all a bust." He

starts swinging his arms and legs, doing horizontal jumping jacks, making an angel in the leaves.

Beanhead says, "I have to go."

They let him go, and he walks home, kicking at leaves
as he goes.

The next week, they show the movie anyway, unfinished. Beanhead can't stand this, but there's no time for
an extension. His father says this is what happens when
you agree to collaborate. Mr. Van Arsdale says it's "an
interesting fragment." Rick Labombard loves it.

He draws some grass, and the air balloon lands. He still
hasn't managed to see his house, his bedroom window.
He starts drawing house after house, windows galore,
skyscrapers full of glass squares. Moon glimmers faintly
behind a building. None of these windows is his. He decides to ask someone, and draws a friendly policeman.
The policeman smiles and points him in the direction he
was already going.

Danny and Asher leave the high school after three years;
they've found a college in Illinois that will take them
without a high school degree. It doesn't work out, for reasons Beanhead never fully understands; he's not in touch
with them much anymore. After a year, they're both back
in Cincinnati, enrolled at UC, and Beanhead is on his way
to a good college in the South. Years pass. Danny moves

to California, Asher to Colorado. The three of them lose contact altogether.

In 2003, at his home in Vermont, Beanhead gets word from an old Clock Hill friend that Jessie has died. She was epileptic, and had a seizure in the shower; she drowned. The funeral will be back in Cincinnati, where Beanhead hasn't been in twenty years. He decides to go.

When he walks into the Clock Hill Church, there is Asher standing by the pulpit, ready to speak the eulogy for his twin. He holds a bottle of water to keep his arm from swinging too wildly in its tremors: he has Parkinson's. He does a double-take when he sees Beanhead among the small group of friends in the pews.

Three years later, Beanhead's father dies peacefully in his sleep. Bob Dylan is still going strong, his voice more of a death-croak than ever.

The beanheaded boy draws a window around the moon, and lo, he's home. He makes his bed, lies down, and draws up the covers. A mobile turns and glitters in the moonlight. He lies awake, clutching the crayon tightly.

THE HAROLD POEMS

On the first page of Crockett Johnson's *Harold and the Purple Crayon* we see the eponymous character, a little beanheaded boy wearing footy pajamas, making purple zigzags all over his white world with the crayon in his right hand. There's no mention of parents or siblings or a home life; there's no school, or neighbors, or anything else. He seems to be two or three years old, with a bald baby head and big seeking eyes. All we're told is that "One evening, after thinking it over for some time, Harold decided to go for a walk in the moonlight." Clearly, this is a thoughtful little dude—and a willful one, too: he can just decide to step out into the night on his own. He doesn't seem to have a bedtime—or a bed, for that matter. The one thing he does have is a big purple crayon. Was it a gift? Did someone teach him how to use it? No telling. Harold just is, and he defines himself in two ways. He wants things—like a walk in the moonlight—and he makes them, with his crayon.

Outside, there isn't any moon, so of course he draws one, or half of one, a capital D sans serif, staring from the barest sky. This watchful eye will stay with him from now on. He needs something to walk on, so he makes a path. And not just any path: "he made a long straight path so he wouldn't get lost." The little beanhead is a sensible boy. Almost immediately, though, the long straight path becomes dull. "So he left the path for a short cut across a field. And the moon went with him." Order and boredom, desire and fear. This is how we make things.

Some of Harold's stories never got told. Until now.

Harold Goes to School

They have no purple.
Beige, brown, cream, quince,
kiwi soda, eiderdown,
everything but purple.
He wants to be amenable;
he tries to draw with brown.
But what wants to be brown?
Not even number two.
You know it would be fuchsia
if it could.

         He draws Miss Gray
into debate. She says
purple is too volatile,
purple leads to loose stools,
purple is for trids.
He draws a breath and then
a door and then
a perfect knob.

Back in the book, Harold makes an apple tree, and then a dragon to protect it, and then, when the dragon scares him so much that his crayon hand shakes, he makes a wavy line that turns into an ocean, into which he tumbles. The imagination can be terrifying. Harold nearly drowns, but manages to draw a trim little sailboat, and he makes land on a sandy beach. The beach reminds him of picnics, and that makes him hungry, so he draws a lunch, with nine kinds of pie. But he can't eat it all, so he creates "a very hungry moose and a deserving porcupine" to finish it off, and he walks on.

Harold at the Zoo

Not satisfied with porcupine
or moose that will not fetch,
he makes the sign say Z-O-O,
and purples in the lawn
with gryphon and ouroboros,
murgatroyd and dodo,
titmouse, pandybat, mcrib.
Beyond a stand of tumtum trees
he scribbles the invisibles:
thimblewatts and mairzydotes,
marchessaults and yawps.
He makes a beeline for the bees
and hangs the keeper's coat thereon.
Cages: none.
He feeds his peeps on whiskey seed,
and lo, they leave no scat.

Harold is the Adam of his creation. Like Adam, he wants more.

Harold Builds a Brother

First, he drew a mirror.
He gazed at that good-looking dude
for ever so long:
that toothless smile, those baby blues,
the rakish way he filled a peejay.
He was the bitchinest kid
on the block, and still
he wasn't enough.

He needed someone to pound on,
to share a suburban bedroom with,
someone he could beat at games
and report cards and comportment
until they both grew up and moved away
and saw each other twice a year,
someone who would be a lefty even though
Harold would try to remedy that,
who would play golf and get married
and vote Republican and live down South
and go to church and join AA
and take care of their mother
and keep up with the cousins
and love his kids unquenchably
and make it through chemotherapy
and never never let him go. And so
he drew one of those.

The brother must have been left-handed because he came from a mirror. Once, in the basement, Harold tried to make him into a righty. It didn't take. Sometimes you have to live with what you draw.

And then there were detours.

Harold at the Blind Lemon

He's never had a drink,
but he can't resist the names:
possets, cobblers, flips, and juleps,
slings and toddies, nogs and grogs
and smashes. He draws up a stool
and points to a drink on the board.
The barkeep nods
and brings him a Screaming Baby
on the Beach. The irony
is palpable. He insists
on a straw and sucks his drink down
to that whickering sound, then
wobbles out to the street
where he looks for a girl
who will lay him
over her shoulder
and burp him.

Up on Mount Adams, high above downtown Cincinnati, The Blind Lemon is a temporary moon. But even a bohemian barroom is not enough; there should also be a girl. Harold just wants to get enjambed. And girls turn up in the strangest places.

Harold at the Old Folks' Home

The service girls go nuts for him
They stroke his head they chuck his chin
They pinch his cheeks they cluck and coo
But still this place just reeks of poo

He's come to see his aged gran
She gives him gum she pats his hand
She says she's happy that he came
She calls him by his cousin's name

At music time they sing a song
But all these feebs just get it wrong
They leave out words they gurgle notes
They've all got bullfrogs in their throats

Dinner is soup straight from the can
The chef has never heard of flan
The beverage menu makes him batty
He wants his skinny mocha latte

And then Lights Out? It can't be true
There's still so much he wants to do
Gran says good night my little friend
The service girls say come again

Since it's too early for curfew, our boy rocks on.

Harold Goes Hip-Hop

He's in the house
he is in the house
he is in the in the in the house
little beanhead is in the house

He's on his toes
in his footy peejays
and can he shake it
oh yes he can oh he can can
oh he can shake his can

Is it time for bed?
Not yet! Not yet!
Nicht wahr and nyet!
Not bed! Not yet!

He's the onliest loneliest onliest man
with the purple cran
in his gummy hand
and he's here to shake it shake his can
don't draw no curtains yet.

How did he get so polyglot? The little beanhead gets around. Sooner or later, he had to become a boulevardier.

Harold Goes Oo-La-La

Parlez-vous rendez-vous
Harold of Purple Stick
Once went to Paris to
Dance the can-can.

All of the mademoiselles
Fell for his oversized
Aphrodisiacal
Lavender cran.

Cabernet s'il vous plait
Louis le Roi Soleil
Offered young Harold a
Nice seasoned steak.

But Marie Antoinette
Understood better; she
Axiomatically
Let him eat cake.

Somehow, something breaks down in his body. Too much steak? Too much cake? It can't have been too much oo-la-la.

Harold at the Hospital

He came in like a wrecking ball
He wasn't feeling well
He raised a mighty baby squall
And seven kinds of hell

He kicked he spat he soiled his pants
He threw their toys about
The nurses didn't stand a chance
He put them all to rout

I'm much too young to die, he cried
Or sounds to that effect
But then they took a look inside
And found his lung suspect

They could not tell him why or whence
These things are strange, they said
Unless you take these medicines
Quite soon you may be dead

What could he do but yield to them?
He feared he'd make it worse
He could have torn them limb from limb
But then he'd have no nurse

He took their poison in his arm
It coursed through every cell

And it would bring him grief and harm
Before it made him well

It might not leave him safe and sound
It might just make him cry
But once you're in the world, he found,
You're old enough to die.

The day devolves; the night draws nigh. What little boy
wants to go to bed?

Harold Does Not Go Gentle

His steps are always haunted by the moon;
It warns him as it walks across the sky:
It says his bedtime's coming all too soon.

He draws upon the page a purple rune,
But cannot riddle out a reason why
His steps are always haunted by the moon.

He once was gladdened by the sun at noon;
He watched the shadows gather, fade, and fly.
They say his bedtime's coming all too soon.

He sketches on the sand a mighty dune
And desert birds that make a mournful cry;
They know his steps are haunted by the moon.

He whistles as he walks a little tune
As if a cemetery's passing by.
It says his bedtime's coming all too soon.

He feels as flimsy as an old cartoon.
He hates to hear the simple word goodbye.
His steps are haunted always by the moon.
It says his bedtime's coming all too soon.

But this can't be the last word. So:

Previously, on "Harold"...

He blazed a trail and walked right off
he made some pies he couldn't scoff
he drew a beast to guard a tree
and when it roared fell in the sea
he climbed a hill again he fell
he looked for home but couldn't tell
which one was his he asked a cop
who couldn't say he didn't stop
but went his way beneath the moon
he knew he'd find his window soon
he lived in words but never spoke
the punchline to an untold joke
don't mind what Crockett Johnson said
he'll never ever go to bed

But Seriously

On the way into Atlanta from the airport, keeping his rented Economy model in the far right of five lanes as most of the traffic zoomed past at speeds no one drove back in Maine, Fletcher goggled at the landscape. Once—even in his own lifetime, when he was growing up here—this had been rolling green hills and woods, well outside of the city. Now it was nothing but concrete, glass, and steel. Five freaking lanes! And yet they were all full, even at noon on a Friday. Was there ever a moment when they fell silent, when a human being could actually walk from one side to the other? Not that there was anything to walk to or from—just shiny office blocks and more roads, heralded by thickets of highway signs. On the phone, his brother had urged him to avoid the new mass transit system, MARTA, which had been midwifed by the feds under Jimmy Carter and then strangled by the Reagan people now pumping more money into highways. Seymour reminded him that it was known locally as "Moving Africans Rapidly Through Atlanta." One of those jokes that might have been funny for a second, before you realized how racist it was. His brother never

o the local newspaper as "The Urinal-Con-
cause that was such a clever play on The
stitution.

This weekend of all weekends Fletcher didn't
dwell on the lameness of Seymour's sense of
humor. He was jetting in for his little brother's wedding,
and he, Fletcher, was the Best Man. This was a time to stay
upbeat. A time to celebrate Seymour and his bride, and
the future, and blah blah blah. But God, were the newly-
weds really going to stay here in this soulless place? Yes,
sure, the whole family came from Georgia, originally;
Seymour liked to say that this was their ancestral home.
Fletcher was the renegade, living in the frozen Yankee
north. Even this morning, the first of May, there had been
frost on his little back lawn outside of Portland. The fore-
cast for Monday, when he had to be back there to monitor
final exams, called for a "winter weather event." A nice
way to send new graduates out into the world: here's
your diploma, watch your step on the ice. Maybe a little
southern weather would be welcome. But how could
anyone call this concrete labyrinth home? More highway exchanges whizzed past. More cars, more asphalt,
more glaring green signs leading nowhere he wanted to
go. The car radio was tuned by default to WSB. Welcome
South, Brother.

Back when he was born here, thirty years before, Atlanta was hardly more than a provincial crossroads, home
to a sleepy genteel tradition, no one's idea of a metropolis.
What had happened to that Old South? In the space of two

decades, air conditioning had changed everything. People moved in from everywhere—Mexico, Asia, dying Rust Belt cities, dusty Georgia towns that had been stranded by the interstate. Towers sprouted. Farms became suburbs. Woods became suburbs. Formerly separate towns became suburbs. The Old South became a restaurant called Aunt Pittypat's Porch, featuring cornbread and sweetened iced tea. Carter's presidency was supposed to signal the rise of the New South, an end to the long national nightmare. What we got in its place, while the concrete hardened, was a long national nap. In a cardigan. Now Reagan was promising an end to our malaise—and the speculators, unbridled, were going wild on towers and highways. When was change ever good?

He pulled into the Comfort Lodge, in a semi-urban no-where not far from the wedding church. Everyone was staying there. His parents' new condo certainly couldn't accommodate him, and this was fine by Fletcher; it wasn't home, anyway.

The receptionist had a big head of dark Charlie's Angels hair, bouffed to the max, and a mouth full of teeth so earnest it hurt to look at her. Her chicken-fried accent was so deep, so drawly, he wanted to pull words out of her mouth with both hands. He knew he shouldn't conclude that a southern accent means you're stupid: it had taken him years, after moving north for graduate school, to extirpate his own. She couldn't have been much older than Fletcher. Maybe she was younger; he was starting to have trouble reading odometers. She said his room would be ready soon, if he'd just take a seat in the sad little "hospitality area" by the front door. The whole place reeked of chlorine from the obligatory swimming pool behind the glass wall just past Miss Elocution's counter. He picked up a free copy of The Urinal-Constipation, and then, after discovering that it contained virtually nothing but local news, searched in vain for a recycling bin. Hello? Trees are a renewable resource? But only if you bother to recycle? He watched a ruddy overweight guy in sweatpants and running shoes toss a paper in the trash, and he wanted to shout. Eventually he stuffed his own miserable hunk of newsprint into his hanging bag. He'd take it back to New England if he had to.

Thank God for New England. It was funny, now, to remember that at first it was just an escape from The Miranda Debacle. He hadn't even been sure that he wanted to go to graduate school — he hadn't been sure of anything — but when the University of Southern Maine offered him a teaching fellowship right out of college, he hightailed it up there in double time. The very idea that someone would pay him for talking with young people about books seemed like the world's greatest scam. And it was. They measured grad students by the year — 1G, 2G, 3G, and so on — and now he was fast approaching double digits. But what was he supposed to do? There weren't any jobs — at least, nothing better than the one he had, teaching sections and hanging out in town and renewing his position year by year until he had a kind of untenured authority just because he had been around so long. He was near the top of the tree. It was a Charlie Brown Christmas tree, but still, the top was the top.

Now here was his younger brother, who had held out for a while, getting married at the age of 28. And he, Fletcher, was still, perpetually, on the cusp. On the cusp of what, he couldn't say. But he was on it.

In the cocktail hour before the rehearsal dinner, his father urged Fletcher to join a church group for young adults, because that was how Seymour met his bride—at a Bible study group that took place every Sunday night. They were standing by a high round formica-top table in a function room at the church, a huge concrete fortress containing a warren of such rooms, all outfitted in beige carpet and framed inspirational posters. "Open your heart to Him," said the text beyond his father's shoulder, over a glowing sunset beach. "Cocktail hour" was a bit of a misnomer; they were in a church, after all. Fruit punch was the best they could do.

"Young adults, Dad? Really? Isn't that like 13 to 15? I'm afraid I may have passed over into the next bracket—you know, Adult Adult. Unadulterated adult."

"I'm sure they don't check your birth certificate at the door, Fletcher." His father, a tall circumspect salesman with a neatly kept crewcut, had been twenty-two when he married Fletcher's twenty-two-year-old mother. "You don't want to wait too long," he said. "It's more fun to grow up along with your kids."

My kids, thought Fletcher. Imagine the poor buggers competing with me for the Cap'n Crunch. They wouldn't stand a chance.

"So," he said, "You want me in there robbing the cradle? Cruising the coeds? Squeezing the fresh produce?"

"Girls like a slightly older man, son. Someone a little more mature. You know, girls tend to grow up faster. They're ready to be serious before the guys their own age."

"Yeah, that's what I'm worried about." It killed him when his father called him "son."

"What?" His father shook the ice cubes in his empty punch glass.

"Nothing. I'm sure you're right." Fletcher had learned long ago that this was the best tactic with his father: suggest vaguely that his advice sounds good, and then do nothing about it. He had seen his father work this strategy on his mother forever. His father nodded, and then snapped into social mode as another wedding guest approached.

At the rehearsal dinner, Fletcher told the one about being a Frisbeetarian. The Best Man was supposed to give a toast, after all. If you could call raising a glass of cranberry juice a toast. "We believe that when you die, your soul goes up on the roof, and you can't get it down." This got a polite titter from the cute bridesmaid seated next to him at the head table, but the rest of the room was unresponsive. Maybe he had misgauged his audience. Most of the men were wearing navy blazers with sky-blue shirts and yellow ties; the women were draped in pastels. Perhaps they were wondering what such a joke had to do with their friend, his little brother, who would be getting married the next day. Maybe a few people were concerned that the Fellowship Hall of Druid Hills All-Faith Church wasn't the right venue for jokes about religion. Maybe they were right. But what the hell. He went on to the one about Joseph, Mary, and Pinocchio—and in a moment of devil-may-care bravado, he told the X-rated version. The church hall fell quiet. The cute bridesmaid looked away. Immediately to his right, he noticed the dandruff on the dark lapels of the father of the bride.

Maybe this was why Fletcher himself was still unmarried? Everyone likes a joke, his father liked to say, but nobody loves a joker. Of course, his father's idea of humor was Bob Hope entertaining the troops. And his mother— well, his mother was a sweet and saintly woman, but she couldn't tell a joke to save her life. No, if this whole sad rigmarole of Seymour's wedding was going to rise above lethal cliché ("We know you and Cindy are going to be great together, we love you so much, just keep on doing what you're doing"), it was up to him. Maybe he shouldn't have thrown in that jape about how his brother was finally going to See More—"as if he hasn't been seeing it all for about three years now." People don't seem to go for sex jokes at the rehearsal dinner. What was wrong with people?

Only one way to find out: pour it on harder. After all, what's a toast that doesn't include a roast? Who doesn't appreciate a little scurrilous irony? Well, to judge by the All-Faith crowd, just about everyone. He told them how his brother had, after a non-sectarian childhood, become a cracker's cracker. Their mother, he said, had always taught them not to say "ain't" or "might could," as in "I might could do that," because there was a difference between being southern and being ill-bred. "But my little brother," he said, "when he came back from college in the north, started saying 'y'all' and 'I reckon' and 'It don't make no never mind' as if he had been given an infusion of grits." He paused. "All that mushmouth talk just makes me want to go nuke-ular."

Nobody laughed. Should he say it again, louder? No, he told himself: when you're on thin ice, skate faster.

So maybe the bit in which he warned Cindy about wet spots on the bed was a tad much. "But everybody goes through a bedwetting phase, right? Am I right?" Cindy's face had been frozen in a pained smile for a while now. Seymour wasn't smiling at all. Fletcher understood: his brother had cold feet. That's why they needed some humor here. If it was all deadly serious, poor Seymour would want to run screaming.

The cute bridesmaid seemed to have left the room. Probably needed to powder her nose. He counted on catching up with her the next day, at the reception, in the drinking portion of the evening. You know what they say about girls at weddings.

That night, back at the Comfort Lodge, he warmed up with room-service Rebel Yell while watching the adult channel. Adults did the strangest things.

The ceremony itself surprised him. Not because there was anything unusual about it: it was strictly by the book. What shocked him was his own emotional response. He was prepared to be blasé, recognizing the meaningless ritual as yet another triumph of hope over experience. But when he stood at the altar next to his little brother and the organist goosed the hell out of the wedding march, he almost lost it. Approaching them on the arm of her starchy tuxedoed father, there was Cindy, dark hair rolling over the shoulders of her white gown, dark eyes flashing from under the veil, a vision of promises kept.

"Goddamn!" he said under his breath, and then wondered how loud it had been. He glanced sideways at his brother, who simply smiled. How could he stay so cool?

Fletcher didn't know his future sister-in-law well; after all, he had been up north teaching Shelley while Seymour was busy with Leviticus. But she seemed to know him. When she arrived at the altar, she gave him one quick look that seemed to say, Don't even think about it, Fletcher. He didn't. When the time came, he brought forth the ring in all solemnity, and then stepped away to watch as his brother committed his life to this woman.

After the bride and groom cut the cake, Seymour re-moved Cindy's garter, and made a big production out of trying to throw it directly to Fletcher. Who came up with these rituals? The lore says that whoever catches the garter will be the next one married. But why was Seymour making a big deal out of this? Why care if his brother was married or not? Was it earnest concern for his welfare? Or was it just a desire to have his own choice ratified? The groom was supposed to throw it over his head, so the toss was more or less random, but Seymour lined it up like a long iron, taking aim for his brideless big brother. Fletcher didn't want to play. But he also didn't want to look like a bad sport, and anyway, he was hemmed in by other members of the party; he couldn't escape. When the toss came, and the damn thing hit him square in the chest, he just didn't put out his hands to grab it. He was saved by the cute bridesmaid, whom he had been trying to chat up. It turned out that she was just angling to be in the line of fire, and when the garter went flying she was all over it, popping a button on his vest as she snatched it from his non-grasp. Wasn't this supposed to be just for the males? This chick was apparently not missing any bets.

Seymour looked disappointed. God, he looked just like Dad. Cindy shook her head. Fletcher was only dismayed that the cute bridesmaid was apparently so intent on nuptials. "Nice grab," he said. "The Braves could use you in center."

Miranda had been his one shot to satisfy everyone's matrimonial hopes. They met in college, and even though she had a slight southern accent, she managed it with sly irony. On their first date she told him that she was fifteen years old before she realized that "Damn Yankee" was two words. She thought Jimmy Carter looked like the cat that ate the canary — "For Pete's sake, he's still got feathers in his teeth." And she knew all the words to the songs on "Stop Making Sense." As he walked her back to her dorm that first night, long after midnight, the two of them careered through the quad chanting "Fa fa fa FA fa, fa fa fa FA fa." This was the girl for him.

And indeed she was, through three years of college — laughs, Häagen-Dazs, a shared disdain for Oliver North. But then, the summer before senior year, he took a false step. Or a false step took him. They were visiting her parents at the family home on the Outer Banks, sitting on a wooden bench in a little park in the town where Miranda had grown up. They were eating the best fish and chips he had ever tasted from old newspaper unfolded in their laps. And then he tried out the Frisbee joke.

She didn't laugh, or say anything.

He said, "You know, like a Frisbee? Up on the roof?" It seemed like that joke should go over especially well with Miranda, a lapsed Presbyterian.

She took a sip of her soda. He said, "You remember how Woody Allen got kicked out of college?"

She shook her head.

"On the final exam for his metaphysics course, he looked into the soul of the guy sitting next to him."

She said, "The soul isn't a laughing matter, Fletcher."

Wasn't it? Were some things out of bounds? He had always been an equal opportunity joke-teller, ever since he saw the cartoon of Godzilla crushing Bambi and laughed till he peed his pants. He must have been ten at the time. Was nothing sacred? All right then, let's have a laugh.

"Oh come on," he said. "It's a joke, for God's sake."

"Well, that's just it," she said. "It's not for God's sake."

Whoa. What did they put in the soda here?

"It's just words, Miranda. It's not like sticks and stones, you know. A person needs to laugh."

"A person loves to laugh." She paused. "But some things just aren't fodder for humor, Fletcher. You know? Sometimes, when you cross a certain line, it's just not funny anymore."

Fletcher let that conversation fade, as they sat licking salt and vinegar from their fingers. But he never ceded the point. He didn't get this idea about lines. Lines were for old people, parents and schoolmarms. He intended to keep crossing them whenever they reared their unsightly heads.

That evening, back in the warm kitchen of Miranda's parents, he wondered if they were looking at him with a more territorial glance, as if to say, What are your intentions, son? Maybe that was the problem. Maybe going to visit her on her home turf had awakened some questions about the nature of their relationship. How serious was it? Maybe this stuff about his soul was a kind of test. Fletcher liked tests. But he wasn't sure he wanted to pass this one.

*

Meanwhile, somewhere along the way, Seymour had become a Believer with a capital B. At the reception that night, at a perfectly manicured country club miles from anywhere, Seymour had insisted on saying the grace, and he didn't stint on the Old Time Religion. "In the name of Him Who died on the cross to take away our sins, under the loving eye of His Father, Who provided this wonderful meal, we bow humbly and gratefully, for ever and ever, Amen." Fletcher stole a look over at the Steinmetzes: did they eat Baptist? And wasn't the meal provided by those black dudes in the short white coats who were standing quietly by, ready to carve some more steamship rounds for this universally white congregation? Shouldn't the flock be a bit nervous about the long knives?

When did Seymour become such a Holy Roller? Somehow this wasn't the kid he remembered growing up with, sharing a suburban bedroom with, watching "The Man from U.N.C.L.E." with on Friday nights in the basement playroom. That kid was a little hell-raiser, always up for an escapade in the woods behind their house—a little too wild for the young Fletcher, in fact. When Seymour got caught filling neighborhood mailboxes with cherry bombs in the company of the well-known rapscallion Jack Johnson—you just knew that kid was no good, he wore white jeans—Fletcher thought it served him right. And, truth to tell, he was a little bit jealous, too.

Boys were supposed to be rapscallions. Somehow young Fletcher had been too skeptical even then for anything like rapscallitude.

At the end of the grace he crossed himself and said "Good wine, good meat, good God, let's eat." The cute bridesmaid giggled nervously. It turned out she was the Maid of Honor, his counterpart in this whole shebang. When he made a crack about her honor, she giggled some more. Her well-lacquered bangs bounced above her eyebrows like the prow of a glamorous ship. He refrained from asking "On her or off her?" He wasn't that dumb.

And then he got badly drunk. It wasn't his fault: this always happened with red wine, and wine was all they were serving. What was he supposed to do, drink white? No way in hell. After the dinner, when people started dancing, he may have gotten a little too forward with Maid of Honor during a slow dance. The band played "Put Your Head on My Shoulder," and she did. On his. It felt good. Those were her boobs against his chest. What a wonderful thing, he thought, boobs against your chest. That was her midsection against his midsection. The crepe of her ridiculous pink bridesmaid dress whispered. So obviously she started it. He may have engaged in a little grinding; he may, when she pulled away suddenly, have tried to blow the bangs off her forehead with a big vinous puff. He just wanted to see them fly; they were so cute. He may have tried the "on her or off her" line then; later, he couldn't remember for sure. Everything got a bit fuzzy. But he was pretty sure that was when she slapped him—a full roundhouse right that rattled his teeth and made a resounding whack in the Fellowship Hall. The Braves could definitely use her in the lineup.

People stopped dancing. The band stopped playing. Fletcher caught a glimpse of his sainted mother standing with Cindy's parents, mortified within an inch of her life.

"Red wine!" he cried. "What was I supposed to do?"

Maid of Honor stalked off, probably headed to the ladies' room to vent her indignation to someone who would understand. That's what girls tend to do. Fletcher wheeled—as well as he could wheel, in his current condition—and strode off the floor, out the door, into the parking lot. That's what guys do.

It was a sticky-warm early-summer night. Didn't this place ever cool off? He pulled off the jacket of his monkey suit, and looked for his car. Something told him, You ain't drivin', son, and he decided to listen. Getting the car key in the lock was too complicated—damn rental car—so he hung his jacket on the antenna. It looked jaunty there.

He was feeling jaunty, too. Nothing like a little whack to wake a fellow up. He hitched up his monkey-suit trousers, loosened his big stripey tie, and lit out for the territory. There had to be something good out there.

But God, there were a lot of cars. And the sidewalk was so narrow. Narrow and curving, like it had been laid out by someone who never took trigonometry. Like it was winding through the woods in The Wizard of Oz. He developed a little hitch in his step, like he had Dorothy and those other dudes at his side. "We're...off to see the Wizard ..."

There was no telling how far he walked. Miles? Leagues? This city had no landmarks; it was just cars and buildings, buildings and cars. It must have been a little while, because the sidewalk straightened out; he must have passed from Curvetown to Lineville. Was this still Druid Hills? He wanted to meet a druid. Where would you find a druid on a Saturday night?

Just ahead, on his right, a brightly lit sign proclaimed an establishment called "Beast of Bourbon." Fletcher nodded. "Now you're talkin'," he said to the night.

In a previous life, this big cinder-block building might have been a meat-processing plant or an auto chop-shop, but now it was a cavernous bar. When Fletcher walked in, he was blasted by the sound system: "So good! So good! I got YOU!" shouted James Brown. Yes, you do, thought Fletcher. As his eyes adjusted to the dark room, he noticed something unusual: it was still warm in here. No air conditioning! It felt like the same janky air had been brewing in this room since about 1958. He liked it. He unbuttoned his vest.

At the periphery of the room, people were hunched over little tables in twos and fours, eating BBQ-by-the-pound off of trays lined with butcher paper. Most of them seemed to be drinking from forties in brown paper bags. Many of them were black. The whole place was fragrant with the smell of charred pork and molasses. Fletcher wondered if he was unwelcome, if he should feel uncomfortable. But what the hell, he'd been in rough bars back in Portland. If he was unwelcome, someone would have to tell him so. From the back of the room came the pock of billiard balls on three or four tables under the haze of hanging metal lamps. Those rectangular islands of green gleamed like a distant promise. Fletcher sidled up to the horseshoe-shaped bar in front and studied the drink list. He went for a Catdaddy corn whiskey. It tasted like bubblegum cough syrup with a kick. James Brown kept on shouting. He felt good.

What was wrong with people? Why couldn't they take a joke? Why was everyone so damn touchy? He wanted to say to the world, Lighten up. Life is too short. In the nineteenth century, people believed in God because they had to. Many women died in childbirth; so did their children; surgery was done with no anesthetic; life expectancy was like forty. It was just too horrific not to cling to some Divine Being, Someone Who would make things all right. But now? Now they had novocaine! Now they had Catdaddy! Lighten up, world!

The music shifted to Ike and Tina Turner. But what the hell? Tina was wailing, the bass was rumbling, the guitar went wacka-wacka just as you expect from Ike and Tina — but the song was "What a Friend We Have in Jesus." Jesus, thought Fletcher. Shadrach, Meshach, and Abednego! Even in this temple of godless consumption, he couldn't escape the Bible-thumpers. Well, they did call it soul music.

What was the soul? The part of us that outlives the body, said Miranda. But how did she know? This was the last time they hung out, September of their senior year. They were back at college, sitting at The Bandersnatch, which used to be their favorite dive. Now it just felt like a college bar. Having your shoes stick to the floor had somehow lost its charm.

"I don't know," she said. "Nobody knows. But don't you want to bet on the possibility? If you bet that we do have a soul, and you're right, you have everything to gain. If you bet that we don't have a soul, and you're right, what do you win? Nada."

He felt his skin tighten. This part of the conversation was like the first thirty seconds out of a hot shower on a cold morning: you know it's going to be a pain, but you just have to get through it. Then you'll be okay.

"I see what you're doing there," he said, with a flourish of his glass. "You're employing logic. I never thought you'd stoop so low."

"But seriously, Fletcher. I worry about you."

"Why? What's the worry?" He took a sip. "That I'll crack one joke too many, and get sent straight to hell?"

Miranda was silent. Tony Orlando shook his hair on the jukebox. My God, thought Fletcher. That *is* what she worries.

"Well," he said, "I'm betting God has a wicked sense of humor. I'm going all in on it. But just to be safe, I always tip big—because He would."

She sighed. A friend of hers stopped by their booth to chat. Next day, he started applying to graduate schools.

Since then, his love life had been motel matches. He struck it lucky from time to time, but nobody was Miranda.

He ordered another Catdaddy. He was getting more

sober. Soberer. More soberific. What if heaven was a place where you couldn't crack wise? It couldn't be. It was unfathomable. Inflammable. Infamatory. Unfathomabobble. He tossed a mental coin.

"All right then," he said out loud, to no one in particular, "I'll go to hell."

Fletcher was never quite sure how he got back to the Comfort Lodge that night. In one memory, he was accompanied by a long-legged Dixie filly who spoke without a trace of an accent. In another, he floated on a Catdaddy cloud, far above the beautiful headlights on the highway. More probably, it was achieved by some combination of muscle memory and dumb luck.

Dumb luck didn't tuck him in, though. His wake-up call the next morning found him still in the monkeysuit trousers, unbuttoned vest, and loud stripey tie, lying outside the covers of the still-made bed, a plastic-wrapped welcome mint stuck to his cheek. On the phone, it was Miss Elocution from the front desk. He'd never heard such vowels in "Good mornin'!"

Who reserved his damn flight for 8 am? Oh yeah, that was him. He grabbed his hanging bag and buttoned his vest—except for the button popped off by Maid of Honor. Ah, good times. And his jacket? Oh yeah: the car antenna. It would help him find the car. He was a genius.

Downstairs in the lobby at 6:30, there was no one but Miss Elocution. It was Sunday morning, after all. Behind its wall of glass, the swimming pool gleamed and flashed. Imagine going for a swim at this hour. You'd drown for sure.

First, drink some coffee. That was his Hippocratic oath. There was a giant metal urn in the hospitality area, smelling like it had been brewed last Tuesday. What the hell: it was hot, it was caffeine. He filled a Styrofoam cup. At least he didn't have to worry about recycling: this thing would still be around when he was ashes and dust. He looked for cream. There was no such of a thing. Instead, there was a cylindrical cardboard container of powdered "creamer." Of course. He held his breath and glunked a cloud of the stuff in his cup. No turning back now.

There was just ten minutes before he had to hit the highway. Somehow, though, he didn't feel like leaving. He looked at The Urinal-Constipation and thought of his brother. Oh, he had some 'splainin' to do.

He walked over to the receptionist's counter, and she looked up from her paper. Her dark curls looked less bouffant this morning. Maybe it was human too.

"Honey," she said, "Whose little boy are you?"

His heart longed to answer, Why, yours.

Sometimes in the Night

Once there was a happy family that lived in a big house in the woods. Father mother sister brother brother brother. The master bedroom was on the ground floor, and the kids all lived upstairs. The sister and the older brother had their own bedrooms, and the two younger brothers shared a room. Theirs was the biggest, with windows on three sides that looked out into the woods. On a bright summer day, it was like living in the trees.

At the foot of the stairs, there was a grandfather clock. It had a bronze face, and above it were images of the moon in its phases. When the family first got the clock, the father wound it up with care so the chimes would ring when they should. The middle brother didn't understand the moon images, which changed throughout the month. He just wanted the time of day. Each quarter hour, the clock sang a musical chime that got longer as it moved toward the top, when it tolled the hour in a bronze and sleepless voice.

The sister did girl things, whatever girls do. The three

brothers played football in the sliver of yard surrounded by trees. The older brother always played quarterback, sending each of his brothers out on pass patterns against the other. He drew the routes on their skinny chests. "Do a buttonhook!" "Run a flare around the tree!" "Go long!" The middle brother ran the best patterns; he liked the word "buttonhook." He always won. Of course, the older brother won either way, since he was on both teams. But the younger brother always lost.

The middle brother did well in school. He loved his fourth-grade teacher, who read *Charlotte's Web* to them every day before lunch. He put his head down on his desk and lived in that barn stall. He wrote little stories of his own, and basked in the praise of his teacher. The little brother didn't do so well. At the dinner table the father quizzed him on spelling;. "Sound it out!" the father said. The little brother tried, but how do you sound out "water"? W-o-d-e-r. The parents decided he should repeat the second grade. The middle brother raced ahead into fifth grade, ramping.

Still, the two younger brothers got along well. When the weather was bad, they played in the basement play-room, which had a map of the world on the wall and a big black-and-white TV. They weren't allowed to watch TV on weeknights, but on Fridays they gorged on "The Man from U.N.C.L.E.," "The Wild Wild West," and "Mission: Impossible." Sometimes they slept down there, on a daybed with a metal fold-out frame. There was no remote control. When the little brother fell asleep, the middle brother got up and turned off the TV. The screen whickered into a dissolving dot.

In the big bright room upstairs, they played games on the tufty throw rug at the foot of their beds. The middle brother martialed marbles into two armies that clashed in battles on the floor. He always took blue, and the little brother took red. Blue always won. Once, before a winner was declared, the little brother sent the marbles flying off the rug onto the hardwood, under tables and beds, and then it was every man for himself.

Sometimes, at night, the younger brother rocked in his bed. He got up on his hands and knees, and swayed forward and back, all the while still sleeping. He slept so soundly that even though he hit his head repeatedly against the wooden headboard he still did not wake up. In the morning he would have a pink lump just below his hairline. The middle brother lay awake and listened to the bump-bump-bump across the room. Some nights, he got up, went over to the other bed, and put a hand on his brother's shoulder—not to wake him, just to bring him back from wherever he was, so he would lie down and sleep quietly, and the middle brother could sleep, too. He thought the younger brother never knew.

Years passed. The sister left home, as older children do. Her room was left empty, so it would be ready when she came to visit. After school, the older brother took a different bus now, and got home at a different time; he stopped playing with the two younger brothers. The middle brother made up games for them to play in the woods behind the house. They fought against the Mexicans at the big dead tree and made a camp against the Germans in the clearing above St. Gertrude's. Sometimes the younger brother had to be a German or a Mexican, and die screaming as the bullets wiped him out. But he always came back to life in time for dinner.

Upstairs, they played together less often. The middle brother listened constantly to his radio, following the Top Forty. He waited for the new listings every Saturday, and charted the hits of his favorites — first, Herman's Hermits, then The Monkees. At one point The Monkees had six of the top ten songs; the middle brother was thrilled. Then, on one of her visits home from college, the sister brought home "Sergeant Pepper's Lonely Hearts Club Band."

The only record player in the house was in the living room, so they could use it only in the afternoon, before the father came home from work. But the middle brother had received a reel-to-reel tape recorder for his birthday. He set up the little microphone in front of the stereo speaker and recorded the whole album, so he could play it upstairs any time he wanted. He listened to it over and over, sitting on his bed, looking out into the trees. His favorite song was "Lovely Rita." He could make the sound of every guitar and drum, and he knew all the words by heart. He loved all the songs, but he was a little mystified, a little scared, by "A Day in the Life," which ended the album. The voice of the singer seemed to come from the moon. It said a lucky man had made the grade, and a crowd of people stood and stared. Who was this man? How was he lucky? Why were they staring? Then the voice said the man blew his mind out in a car, and the crowd of people looked away, but the voice just had to laugh. It didn't make sense. What did it mean to blow your mind out? Why would anyone laugh? It wasn't at all like "Lovely Rita," but he knew that Paul and John wrote them both. That was part of the magic.

Later that year the middle brother saved up his money and bought "Magical Mystery Tour" for himself. He learned the differences between the singers. That was Paul on the upbeat songs like "Penny Lane"; John sang the strange ones, like "Strawberry Fields," which said that nothing is real. And yet sometimes the world felt like that. It made his mind itch in a way he couldn't scratch. Still, he couldn't stop listening.

The little brother didn't have a radio or tape recorder. He didn't need one. Their room was full of music all the time.

One night at dinner, the father announced a change in the household. The older brother would move down to the basement playroom, which they didn't need any-more, now that they were big boys. The middle brother would move into the older brother's upstairs room, and there would be more space for everyone.

The middle brother's new room wasn't big and bright, but it did have a window that opened onto the roof above the kitchen; sometimes he climbed out there, just to take the air. He liked his new room, and covered the walls with posters from the mall — a big Chiquita banana, the Marx Brothers happily smoking a hookah. The father looked at the posters quizzically, but the mother said it was okay. Over the bed were four color photos of the Beatles from The White Album. None of them was smiling. The brothers weren't allowed to wear their hair that long.

The middle brother's new room was a little further along the upstairs hall, closer to the stairs. At night, he started hearing the grandfather clock chiming, as he had never heard it before. He lay awake listening, counting the hours. He rustled the sheets in an effort to drown out the chimes. But still they sang on, and he lay in wait for the next one. When he complained, the father said he was being too sensitive; you could get used to anything.

The older brother left home, as older children do. The two younger brothers no longer played together. The middle brother was busy with student council and the baseball team. Sometimes at the dinner table he learned that the younger brother had got in trouble for his grades, or for hanging out with the wrong kids. Once they put cherry bombs in mailboxes up the street, and the younger brother was grounded. The middle brother made straight As; he was never grounded.

News came into the house with *Time* magazine, and it was mostly bad. Ghettos were burning. MLK and RFK were shot. More and more body bags came home from the war. The father said that if the older brother stayed in college he wouldn't have to fight the Vietcong.

Then one night in his room the middle brother heard it on the radio: Paul was dead. They said he had died several years before, in a car accident. But Paul was so popular that they couldn't let him die. So they found a look-alike and trained him secretly. That was why Paul, who had always been "the cute one," had become so mournful-looking. That was why "Sergeant Pepper" started with a song that introduced a new singer, "the one and only Billy Shears." Paul blew his mind out in a car, and no one was smiling.

The radio said there were too many clues to ignore. At the end of "Strawberry Fields" there was a muffled voice that said, "I buried Paul." If you played "Revolution 9" backwards, it said "Turn me on, dead man" over and over. On the cover of "Abbey Road," John led the procession across the crosswalk in a white suit, like a holy man; Paul's stand-in came last, the only one going barefoot, the only one out of step. The radio said this meant that he was being led to his funeral. The license plate on a parked car said "28IF": Paul would have been 28 if he had lived.

That night the middle brother lay awake for hours. He wasn't supposed to believe in ghosts. The clock sang its chimes all night long. There was nothing he could do. He got up and stood at his window, where he saw the moon shining through the trees. Finally, he crept out into the hall, and into the younger brother's room.

He knew his brother slept in the bed furthest from the door. In the dark, he pulled back the cover of the other bed, his old bed, and lay down there. He would get up early in the morning and slip out, smoothing out the bed-spread carefully. He thought the younger brother would never know. He listened to his brother's steady breath-ing. Soon he was asleep.

This was long ago. In time, the two younger brothers left that house, as older children do. They went their ways; they made their lives. They got in touch a couple of times a year.

John is gone now. The father is gone. The younger brother, inexplicably, is gone. Death doesn't explain. Sometimes in the night the middle brother lies awake and listens to the voices. The radio says everything dies; there are too many clues to ignore. The moon says noth-ing is real. The clock says you can get used to anything. Sometimes, he could swear, he feels a warm hand on his shoulder.

ULTRA-BOY AND MARIE

"So," he says, "You're really moving out."

"Marc," she says. "We've gone over this."

It's the week before Christmas, and they're on the road to Montreal. He's driving. They left before dawn, so she can get to her early afternoon appointment. It's still dark, and the interstate is oddly quiet. Maybe everyone is already home for the holidays. Maybe nobody in their right mind would be driving north at this time of year. But if you want to have laser surgery on your eyes in the Year of Our Lord 1999, you still have to go to Canada; the FDA has not yet given its blessing. Back in New York, Jamie will be moving in with her boyfriend on January 1.

"So why isn't he making this trip with you, instead of yours truly?"

"You know he can't get away on a weekday."

"Right. These are billable hours."

"If he's going to make partner, he can't just take off. Especially at this time of year. The year-end crush is insane."

"Right." He scratches his belly. She hates it when he does that. It means he's pissed off, but he's trying not to say so.

"Besides, you're my expert on all things Montreal."

"True." He grew up in a scruffy eastern township, but he hasn't been back there in years.

"And of course you're the man with the Vulva."

"So I am." That's what he calls the old Volvo that is now sailing up the dark highway. He's the only person in her speaking acquaintance with a car, which is so difficult to maintain and park in the city — but he keeps it just for occasions like this. Even a die-hard transplanted New Yorker sometimes needs to get out of town.

"Could it be," he adds, "that he doesn't really want you to get this surgery?"

"He says it's fine with him. I mean, he says he loves me just as much with glasses, but if this is what I really want, then I should do it. He's paying for it, after all."

"Like he'll even notice it on the credit card bill. So why are you doing it, if The Baby Man is just as happy with you wearing glasses?"

"Because I've worn glasses forever. I want to wake up in the morning and be able to see." She gazes out at the highway lights, haloed by cold. "I remember when I first got glasses at age eleven, when I was flunking fifth grade because I couldn't see the blackboard, and my father took me to the eye doctor, and on the way home, in the car, suddenly I could see everything — license plates and birds in the trees we passed — this whole world I didn't even realize I had been missing. Don't you wish for a transformation like that?"

He doubts she was flunking fifth grade, but he lets it go. "Nope. I've had enough transformation for one lifetime. I'm sticking with ye olde Status Quo."

"Besides," she says, "you have no idea what a pain it is for a dancer to be as blind as I am. God knows you can't wear glasses on stage, because that's not the image of the girl in the tutu, or even the girl who's playing a splash of paint in The Jackson Pollack Story."

He laughs. "Jack the Dripper. I loved that."

"And my eyes just won't tolerate contacts anymore; they're constantly red and tired, and I'm so sick of all the apparatus, the fluids and the lost lenses and the eye appointments. But I can't just go on stage without them, either—believe me, I've tried. If you keep missing your mark and bumping into the prima just when she's about to start the pas de deux, she is not amused."

"But aren't you giving up all that? Isn't that the whole idea of moving in with The Baby Man?"

"Don't call him The Baby Man."

"But that's what he is. The Baby Maker. He's going to make an honest woman of you, and put a baby in your belly, and then you'll never dance again."

"Well," she says. And then she doesn't say anything else for a while. Near the Poughkeepsie exit, there are still piles of crusty plowed-up snow, gleaming in the highway lights. She squints through her stylish midtown frames. She's never been up here before, and she was hoping for a little winter wonderland. "Maybe it's time, you know? I'll be thirty-five in June. That's not impossible for a first baby — I've studied the statistics —"

"I'm sure you have. You are nothing if not thorough."

She gives him a look, like Whatever. What was she thinking when she let him see all those ledgers in her teenage journals? All those lists — calories consumed, calories expended, rankings of boys in her high school, bowel movements, orgasms, Times That Tommy Flanagan Spoke to Me... Well, she was thinking that's what you do when you share an apartment with someone: you open up. Was that so wrong?

"Lots of women do it this late," she says. "But the chances of birth defects grow with every year. Anyway, I've known Cedric for two years. Don't I know enough about him by now? He loves children. You should see him with Holly's kids. If it's not going to be Cedric, then I'd have to start all over, you know?"

"You know how I feel about monogamy."

She knows. He tells her anyway.

"People talk about certain birds, like geese, that mate for life, as if that made them the paragons of the animal kingdom. As if they weren't chained for life! How many lives do you get?"

He never talks about Robert, whom he lost in the plague, back in his Montreal days. She just knows that Robert was not welcome in his parents' home, and Marc never forgave them. After Robert's death he left for New York, like so many people, to start again. He didn't attend his father's funeral. Sometimes his mother calls the apartment, and Jamie makes nice on the phone, which pisses him off.

He's still muttering. "Freakin' geese."

"I don't want an anonymous donor, Marc."

"I know you don't. You don't even want The Sperminator." He gestures at his own crotch. "Which is standing by, if you ever change your mind. But no, you want a Baby Man, not someone who will be out at the Caballero all night. Which is where I will be, baby. But really, Cedric?"

"What's wrong with Cedric?"

"Well first of all, there's his name. What were his parents thinking? He doesn't want a Cedric Junior, does he? Or no, no, Cedric the Second, with Roman numerals? Because that would be tragic."

"We just want a baby, Marc. We could name it Adolf for all I care. But I think the first one is going to be a girl."

"Oh, lovely, a sweet little girl named Adolf. *She* won't have any complexes. So you're already planning on multiple offspring?"

"Well, yeah, I don't want an only child. I know too well what that's like. But I wouldn't push my luck. Two will do. A girl and a boy."

"Little Adolf and her brother Helmut. Have you checked on the bloodline of the Baby Man? Is it acceptably Aryan?"

"Well ..."

"You have, haven't you? I bet you've got it all traced

out, back to some Baron von Ribblesdorfer in the middle ages."

"You can find out anything online."

"Well, we know your Granny Morgan will be happy."

She lets this pass. No use defending the family Nazi.

"So," he says, "What about your current gig?"

"What about it?"

"Are you just going to quit?"

"I don't know. I mean, it's not like I'm prima ballerina at the NYC Ballet."

"No—but you're dancing in New York. How many girls from Franklin, Tennessee can say that? It's what you always wanted to do."

"Well, I always wanted to be Marie in The Nutcracker. But I'm a little long in the tooth for that now. And a little low in the rump."

"Oh, come on, you've got an amazing body. And I'm speaking as someone who doesn't even want to get into your tutu, so you know you can trust me."

"But dancers have different standards! My legs are too short, my hips are too wide, my neck is too thick—"

"Jamie," he sighs. "You know what the best thing anyone ever said to me was?"

"Tell me."

"This was back when I was about fifteen, and I was just starting to explore Montreal on my own, taking the bus into town and hanging around The Plateau, trying to look older than I was. I swear, I learned more French in an afternoon than I had in ten years of mandatory bilingual education at my Anglo school. Anyway, there was this guy in a bar on the rue Ste. Catherine who gave me a good look, like he knew every detail of my life, right down to the 'Funny Girl' poster on my suburban bedroom wall, and he said, 'Tu n'es pas beau, mais tu es passable.'"

"'You're not handsome, but you're passable'? How is that the best thing anyone ever said to you?"

"Handsome guys are intimidating. And they always have to wonder, 'Does he just like me for my looks?'" He laughs. "I don't have that problem."

He lets a little scenery scroll past. Dark pine woods against a paling sky. "Sometimes," he says, "You have to get inside the punch."

"What does that mean?"

"If you stay at arm's length, you're in the sweep of a haymaker. If you get in close, the other guy's less likely to knock you down."

Her latest gig is in "The Notcracker," a knockoff of the famous ballet. One of those zany Brooklyn things. She explains that since she's about twice as old as the Fairy Cavalier, they cast her as the Cougar Plum Fairy.

"Brilliant," he says. "Is the Fairy Cavalier what I hope he is?"

"No! Well, maybe. Okay, probably. Have you even seen The Nutcracker?"

"No. The title always made me uncomfortable."

She smiles. She actually likes it that he knows nothing about dance. It's one of the bases of their friendship. That and the fact that they both like slender, neurasthenic men. "Well, I've done bits in The Nutcracker all my life, everybody does, but I was always one of the Flower girls, or a shepherdess, or one of the gingerbread soldiers—"

"Oh, I would have bought a ticket for that."

"Of course, I always wanted to be Marie, like any little girl, but I knew I wasn't pretty enough—"

"Which is a crock of shit, but go on."

"And now, at almost thirty-five, I get to do this part that makes fun of the whole thing. And it's actually smart, and well choreographed. It's a hoot."

"But isn't it just a Christmas thing?"

"Well, the original is—but parody is eternal. Who knows how long we can go on? I think the audience is full of hipster women who wanted to be Marie when they were young—all those little girls who wanted to see the nutcracker turn into a prince overnight, and beat the hell out of the Mouse King. Now they come to see us take revenge on that whole bloated fantasy."

"Wait, there's a Mouse King? You interest me strangely. What does he do?"

"He just comes out of the woodwork. It's Christmas Eve, and there's a big party, and the kids all get special gifts—Marie gets this beautiful nutcracker in the shape of a military commander, and her brother gets a whole troop of gingerbread soldiers—and then, after they're sent to bed, she can't sleep, so she gets up to check on the nutcracker, and suddenly there's this giant mouse with seven heads, and a crown on every head—"

"Seven heads? This is getting better all the time."

"Don't laugh. I bet those comic books you were reading were way weirder."

"Hey, don't knock Ultra-Boy. Anyway, what happens with the Mouse King?"

"He starts attacking Marie, along with this whole battalion of mice, and the nutcracker comes to her defense, with the gingerbread soldiers, and there's this big battle—"

"What are the mice going to do, nibble them to death?"

"Basically. The soldiers have cannons that fire hunks of cheese at the mice, but they start to get the upper hand anyway, and the Mouse King zeroes in on the valiant Nutcracker, and wounds him, and everything is looking really bad, but then Marie, who's been watching all this in dismay, takes off her slipper and throws it at the Mouse King, who's distracted just long enough for the Nutcracker to give him a fatal stab with his sword."

"Don't tell me: the Nutcracker turns into a handsome prince, and they get married, and they all live happily ever after."

"Well, first there's this whole long phantasmagoria in which they travel to the Land of Sweets, which is ruled by the Sugar Plum Fairy, and they're entertained by Arabian Coffee and Spanish Hot Chocolate and Candy Canes from Russia—which has nothing to do with the plot, but Tchaikovsky has a great time with all the musical stereotypes. And then yes, it's happily ever after. With a sugar headache. Near the end, the Sugar Plum Fairy whispers something to Marie, but we never find out what she says. I've always thought it was 'Don't ever die.'"

"Okay, so you've got this great gig. How could you just quit? Is The Baby Man putting the pressure on?"

"No. Well, okay, a little. He doesn't see why I'd want to keep doing this. It's not like it pays a lot."

"And you can't stay with it if you're going to have little Adolf in the oven."

"Right."

"But it's dance! In New York!"

"Yeah, but how long can I do it? Daddy always said, Do not become an athelete—you have to give it three syllables, Tennessee-style— because first of all that's not for girls, and second, they're burned out by thirty-five and then they got nothin' but memories and bourbon."

"So you're quoting your father now?"

"He wasn't always wrong. He didn't want me to get the butterfly tattoo, either."

"Well, he was right about that. Still ..."

"You just don't want to lose The World's Best Roommate."

"You laugh, but you never met the whole parade of Roommates from Hell who came before you. Talk about things coming out of the woodwork. Just because it's a decent two-bedroom on the West Side, and it's rent-controlled, and nobody knows about our little cockroach issue... And for God's sake, Jamie, it's the week before Christmas—which you know I hate anyway—and I've got to interview potential roommates now? Or get thrown out because I can't afford the rent as of New Year's Day? I swear, Y2K is going to be the end of me."

She has never quite fathomed his financial situation.

He does something with baskets of specialty foods that get sold at upscale places like Dean & DeLuca, but it's a boom-or-bust market: some months everybody's crazy for his gingko and packets of chai spice tea, and then the next month nobody's buying, and he sits around the apartment muttering things like "Mortadella? Artisan fruitcake?" If she didn't get that monthly bump from Granny Morgan, they would definitely have had some desperate stretches. She'll be paying for the hotel room tonight—which is only right, since he's doing her such a favor. Good thing they don't need two rooms; it's not like they have any secrets. Cedric is fine with it, since Marc is no threat. Of course, he doesn't know that Marc always sleeps in the nude—but why would that matter?

"Oh, you'll find somebody. It's a great apartment. You're just worried because the next person won't make such fabulous grilled cheese sandwiches."

"I still don't know how you do it."

"It's a Tennessee thing. I will take the secret to my grave."

"And who's going to do my laundry?"

"Oh, poor baby. You'll have to go all the way down to the basement by yourself."

"Hey, you never know what might be lurking down there. It's like those old maps where they marked the unknown territories 'Here Be Dragons.'"

"How would you know? You haven't been down there in two years."

"Well, you said you didn't mind."

"I don't. The stairs are good exercise."

"See? How could I ever find someone like that?" He looks over at her so long that she worries about his attention to the road. "And who," he asks, "is going to make sure I get enough water when I'm, um, a little dehydrated?"

She always carries a Nalgene: water is her secret to keeping trim. That, and eating almost nothing. Whereas he, on a good day, looks like Dylan Thomas in his cups, and acts like him, too. He likes to call himself The Camel: he says you never know when the next oasis will appear, so you'd better drink now.

"I'm just going to be across town, Marc. It's not like I'm dying."

"It's worse! The East Side is where fun goes to die! You'll be eating in those faux-French bistros where they put a tiny dollop of nothing in the middle of a big white plate, and you'll be taking little Adolf to pre-pre-pre-school in her BMW pram! You'll never come out to the Caballero anymore!"

"You just don't want to go there on your own. It's always so handy for you to have a partner in crime while you scope out the possibilities. Do you know how many times I've walked home alone from that dive?"

"Oh, don't pretend that you won't miss it."

"I will. But there's no future in it, Marc."

"Future," he mutters, and gazes out at the monochrome landscape. It's late morning now, but it's one of those days when daylight never quite materializes; the horizon is a gauzy haze. "The future is overrated."

He scratches his belly. "So?" he adds. "What are you gonna do?"

"I've told you. I'm moving in with Cedric. I'll figure out the dance thing later. First, I'm getting my eyes fixed."

When they get to the border, Marc goes quiet. He has told her how easy it will be—they don't even ask for ID—but she can feel his nervousness. He has told her the story about the one time he came back, to visit some friends. He got a big fat ticket for parking outside some bar in Vieux Montreal, and he didn't pay it, and when they sent him the threatening reminder a few weeks later, back in New York, he said, "What are they going to do, send the Mounties after me?" So he never paid it, and now it's been a few years, and probably it's lost in the system, but hey, you never know, they could just be waiting until he tries to enter the country again. The Canadians are supposed to be mild-mannered and all, but he says you don't want to cross them. They could impound the Vulva, and throw him in an oubliette in deepest Saskatchewan.

Since he's in the driver's seat, he's the one being interrogated. He explains their purpose. The customs man, a big ruddy guy with long sideburns, perks right up.

"Oh, the laser thing? We're getting a lot of those lately. Those guys must be raking it in. My wife wants to do that. Man, you couldn't pay me enough. To have somebody cut into your eyes? Holy jeez. No offense, ma'am."

He leans in to give Jamie a sympathetic glance. She smiles and thanks him for his concern.

"Actually," Marc says, "It's not like a knife or anything. It's just a beam, perfectly calculated to reshape your cornea, presto change-o."

The guy is frowning at his screen. Marc says, "So, is your wife going to do it?"

The guy looks up. "Huh? Not on my watch, bud." Then he says, "Have a nice stay, folks."

"God, what a wasteland," Marc says, as they cruise into southern Quebec. "Did you notice what happened when we crossed the border? We were on this nice American interstate, with bosky Vermont hills on both sides of the road, and then as soon as we hit Quebec it turns into this two-lane collection of potholes, and suddenly the speed limit is 50, and there's a furniture truck in front of us, and it's impossible to pass, and the landscape is flat as a crepe, and the only scenery is the occasional little one-stoplight town with a convenience store and a strip club. It's like we just got air-dropped into 1950."

She doesn't want to knock his country, so she doesn't say anything. After a while, he starts singing softly to himself.

"Oh les fraises et les framboises, le bon vin que nous avons bu …"

And then he pulls into the parking lot of a one-story cinderblock building that seems to emerge from nowhere after a bend in the road. The movie-marquee style sign outside, with white light bulbs blinking in a rectangle around the black letters, proclaims, "Jeunes Filles Nues."

"Time for a pit stop," he says.

"Really?" she says, as they get out of the car. "Since when are you interested in Young Naked Girls?"

"Hungry," he says. "Sled dog…must…have…food."

Inside, there's a blast of hot, humid air, and then a second blast: country music. "It's your peeps!" he says. She winces. The woman behind the bar is neither young, naked, or, chronologically speaking, a girl; she's fifty if she's a day. Her Santa's elf costume, complete with green velveteen jacket and red-feathered cap, advertises her impressive breasts, which direct them to a table. She seems to be the only person in the joint.

There's no menu, just some soapy illegible scrawls in French on the mirror behind the bar. "In a place like this," he says, "There's only one thing to eat. Fortunately, it's the only thing I want."

"And that is?"

"Poutine! You can't tell me you've never had poutine."

"I've never had poutine. What is it?"

"We'll get you some, and then you'll know."

"But you know I'm not going to eat it. You'll just wind up eating mine."

"And then everyone will be happy."

He orders them two poutiness and two beers. She takes her pill bag from her purse, and lines up several capsules by her water glass. This happens at every meal.

"If you eat your poutine," he says, "You won't need those."

"There is no way you can get enough magnesium or riboflavin from everyday foods," she says. "Unless you eat, like, a ton of nuts."

"So eat a ton of nuts!"

"No way! Do you know how many calories there are in a single walnut?"

"No. Nor do I want to know. More nuts all around, I say."

Soon, the food arrives—two steaming heaps of fries smothered in a gravy that features white lumps of something.

"Curds?" she says, poking at hers. "What are curds?"

"They're delicious, that's what. Eat up. You're a growing girl."

"I am not. I stopped growing twenty years ago. And this weekend I have to look hot as the Cougar Plum Fairy." She tosses back a pill with a gulp of water.

"Come on! It's the Land of Sweets!"

He polishes off his plate, and points at hers. "You going to eat that?"

She sweeps a be-my-guest hand at her plate.

"If you quit dancing," he says as he tucks into her fries, "You can eat anything, right?"

"In theory. But we both know I wouldn't. Hey, listen to this," she adds, nodding at the sound system.

"Twangy," he says, with his mouth full.

"It's Bill Monroe and the Blue Mountain Boys." She sings along. "I saw the light, I saw the light, no more darkness, no more night, now I'm so happy, no sorrow in sight, pra-haise the Lo-hord, I saw the light."

She folds her napkin into a triangle, lowers the point in her water glass, and reaches over to dab at his cheek. "Just a little *shmutz*," she says.

He nods. *Shmutz* is one of those words she got from him, like *mishegas* and *verklempt*, words she can't imagine living without.

"Daddy used to say Bill Monroe was his hero. It wasn't really true—he actually went for elevator music, like 'A Hundred and One Strings Play Bridge Over Troubled Water.' But he liked to pretend he was a hillbilly at heart."

She lets him eat in silence for a while.

"Marc?" she says

"Mm-hm?"

"When did you know you were—you know—"

"A caballero?"

"Yeah."

"Oh, God, haven't I told you that story? I was eleven, and I went to a sleep-over at Steve Bull's house in Sherbrooke, which was way out of my league, I wasn't nearly cool enough for Steve Bull, I mean, he was one of those guys in stone-washed jeans, with his shirt always untucked, you know? No way would my mother let me have a pair of jeans like that, no matter what kind of tantrum I threw at Hudson's. Anyway, somehow I got invited, and it was excruciating. I mean, I untucked my shirt as soon as I got there, but somehow that wasn't enough, you know? All they did was sports, all de live-long day. Touch football that afternoon—and I was godawful, last to be picked for a team—and then the Alouettes on TV that night, and these guys seemed to live and die with each play, you know, and I just looked at them, they were like from another planet—and then foosball in the basement where we were all supposed to sleep, and I was godawful again, who can make those little plastic men do what you need them to do? It's insane. And then all the talk about girls, and it was sports all over again—second base this, and third base that, and I had no idea what they were talking about, and I sat there hoping no one would call on me, you know, like when you just know the teacher is going to nail you on the day after your father showed up with his floozy and kept you awake by fighting all night with your mother."

He washes down the last of the fries with a big slug of beer.

"What was the question again? Oh yeah. That was the moment. I didn't sleep a wink that night. I just lay there in my sleeping bag on that concrete floor—how does anyone sleep like that?—and somehow I knew that this was not my team. That I didn't want to be *on* a freakin' team. The next morning I tucked in my shirt, and I noticed that Rob Miller had his shirt tucked in, too. And I thought, Hmm. And the rest is queer history."

"Where do you think Steve Bull is today?"

"He's probably busy telling his wife she can't get laser surgery. You want to look him up? I bet he's fertile as a rhesus monkey."

The surgery is a breeze. While he sits in the waiting room

reading magazines, she gets her eyes measured with some fancy equipment, and then they conduct her to a dark little room full of more fancy equipment, and they zap her with the beam, twice. There's a faint sizzling sound and an odor of burning hair.

When she comes back to the waiting room, she has a white blindfold taped over her eyes. This is supposed to stay in place for twelve hours, to guard against the temptation to rub her eyes while the incisions "settle."

He says, "Hey, you look like the photographic negative of a raccoon."

"Charming."

"I mean that in the nicest way. A really cute raccoon." Then he adds, "Listen, I've got an idea. You brought some nice clothes, right?"

"Of course. It's not every night I'm in the glamorous capital of French North America."

"All right then. So did I. Let's go to the hotel and get dressed."

"Why? Where are we going?"

"Trust me."

Later, they're at a bar on St. Denis. There's a big bowl of mussels on the table between them. He is in full Camel mode.

She says, "I can't believe you took me to see that."

"Well, you can't say you actually saw anything."

"You know what I mean. You took me to experience that."

"It seemed like the right thing. So? What did you think?"

"It was amazing. I had forgotten how much I love Tchaikovsky. The pas de deux made me cry."

"I noticed. Your mask sprang a leak."

"Well, they warned that my tear ducts would be extra active for the first day or two."

"Right."

"In a way, it was even better not to see the dancing. So how was it?"

"The dancing? You're asking me?"

"I am. How was it?"

"To tell the truth, it was a little poofty. But some of those guys can really rock a leotard, if you know what I mean."

"I know what you mean. And the Sugar Plum Fairy — was she beautiful?"

"That chick was so skinny her heart was standing room only."

She hears the clicking of shells as he helps himself to mussels. "These are fantastic," he says. "Just enough garlic in the butter sauce. You have to try them. I hear they're chockfull of magnesium."

She finds her plate, and holds it in front of her like a little orphan girl. She can feel the tiny plops as the innards of mollusks are dropped on it one by one. He goes on.

"You've got to tell me more about the plot, though. I mean, she gets up to check on the nutcracker doll, right? And then she falls asleep on the divan with it in her arms — nothing sexual about that — and then the next thing you know there's this giant mouse cavorting around, and the gingerbread soldiers are coming to life, and so on — so it's all a dream, right?"

"Well, yeah …"

"But she never comes out of it! The nutcracker turns into a handsome prince, and they stroll off into the forest, and then they're off to the Land of Sweets — and we never see her wake up! She never comes out of the dream!"

"Why would she come out of the dream?"

There's a pause. Techno-pop burbles on the bar's sound system.

"Okay," he says. "But tell me: do they always have the Christmas tree suddenly grow like that?"

"Oh, yeah, that's obligatory Nutcracker staging."

"Well, maybe it's just me, but — that tree shooting straight up through the room? It was just like a massive boner."

She laughs. "It's just you."

"Oh, come on! You should have seen the look on that little girl's face. She was like, 'Come to Mama!'"

"You're disgusting!"

"Aren't I, though?"

"So," she says, "Did the Fairy whisper to Marie?"

"Oh, oui."

"What do you think she said?"

"I think she said, 'Don't forget to separate whites and colors.'"

She throws a shell at him. Even with the blindfold on, her aim is true.

On the street afterwards, he says, "You should see the lights. They really go nuts over Christmas up here."

"I thought you hated Christmas."

"It's growing on me."

"So maybe you'll call your mother?"

"Don't push your luck."

Several hours later, she finds herself lying awake in the dark. Across the little gap between beds, he's snoring like a bandsaw.

She gets up and makes her way slowly to the side of the room away from his bed. Even from behind the blindfold, she can tell where the window is: there's a faint glow. It must be the city lights. Of course he wouldn't have thought to pull the blinds. When he's in Camel mode, he collapses hard.

It must have been twelve hours by now. Carefully, she undoes the tape and peels off the mask. She almost doesn't want to look.

Make Me a Wreck as I Come Back

No one could say for sure when it first appeared. One day in late summer it was just there at the curb, across the street from us, in front of Ruth's house. Elly Taylor said she saw it first, but she was always making claims like that. She said she saw the total lunar eclipse from her top-floor room, although it was completely cloudy that night. There was a break in the clouds, she said, and she was watching because she'd heard on NPR that it would be really special, and she said it was, you should have seen it. Leah and I were watching from our back porch; we listened to NPR, too. And we saw zilch. But it's true that we gave up after a while, because there was no point in watching a sky full of cloud-cover, opaque as obsidian. Elly never gave up. Since Alvin's death a couple of years before, she had devoted herself to watching the block. She could give you a medical report on any of the neighbors—Bud Marriott's knee replacement, Joe Palawczuk's heart condition, Brooksie Graebert's gall bladder. Leah and I called her The Interpreter of Maladies.

Anyway, the bus was definitely there, at the curb in front of Ruth's house, and nobody knew where it came from. It wasn't as long as a classic school bus; maybe it came from a smaller school district. And it definitely wasn't the usual orangey-yellow. This thing was a dusky gray-green, with a matte finish, like they had just put on a primer and never completed the job. Leah said maybe they ran out of money; you know what school budgets are like these days. But did it even belong to a school? There was no writing on the side, just that dark cloudy gray, like camouflage for a night mission.

Ruth didn't seem to care; she had bigger worries that summer. She had been diagnosed with breast cancer in the fall, which meant taking a leave from her job at the college so she could deal with the treatments. The prognosis wasn't good. She was always schlepping back and forth to the hospital, wearing an assortment of colorful wraps and hats on her bald head. They looked pretty good, really—Ruth always went for bright colors, and she could pull them off—but she joked about how the absence of eyebrows made her look like one of those hairless cats. She called herself a chemo sapien. "I'm a whole new species," she laughed, "I'm the undead." And we laughed, too—what else could we do? We left casseroles and custards on her stoop, and she said, "Do you think I'm not fat enough already?" Ruth was a big woman, and she had gained weight in the past six months. All she could digest was white food—cheesy pasta, steamed chicken and rice, milk shakes and ice cream. She called herself QIBIFA—Quite Ill But Inexplicably Fat Anyway. We wished we could do more.

And we wished Harper would do more, too. At least, that's what I wished. Leah always took Harper's side. "Come on," she said as she put the saag paneer in the microwave one night. "The poor kid is fifteen, and her father is God knows where, and now suddenly her mother is going through all this scary stuff, and Ruth doesn't exactly make it easy to help. You've got to feel for Harper."

"No, I don't." I was standing at the counter, chopping up things for my salad. We always had to prepare separate dishes because I was gluten- and dairy-free. "Her mother is going through chemo hell, and the 'poor kid' can't even be bothered to come home for dinner?" Ruth told us that Harper wasn't home much these days; she was always hanging out with friends in the park down the street, or getting rides into town to stand around on the mall. "I saw her in town last week," I said. "I swear she seeks out the sketchiest kids she can find for company. And she was smoking. You know Ruth would hate that."

"Probably. But don't you remember being fifteen?"

That was a low blow. Of course I remembered. Fifteen was when I started dating girls, and my parents weren't exactly thrilled. I guess I didn't hang around our house much in those days, either.

"But my mother didn't have a fatal disease!"

"So you think Harper's life has to stop because her mother's sick?" Leah took her plate to the table; I was still chopping.

"Of course not. I'm just saying she could be around more, that's all." For a while I had been really close to Harper. Mac had taken off when she was thirteen, saying that Ruth wasn't the woman he married anymore. "He means I'm not a hundred and ten pounds anymore," she said. "Hell, I'm almost twice the woman he married!" In those first few months, Harper spent a lot of time with me. She came over after school, because her mother was working—Ruth worked all the time that year—and she often stayed for dinner. I told Ruth we didn't want to create an obstacle between mother and daughter, and she said, "It's better that she's over there with you than sitting like a mushroom with me."

Years before, Leah and I had thought about having a child of our own. Lesbian couples were doing it all the time. We even had a plan: her brother was going to be the father, through artificial insemination. That would have kept both bloodlines intact, and provided fresh purpose for our turkey baster. But then my thyroid thing began, and we put it off, and as time went by we just didn't talk about it anymore. Leah was busy, as usual, at the Community Development Office—and it was good work, making a difference in town. I was at the bookstore— not a career, exactly, but a happy job that helped pay the mortgage. And we had Kinsey, the best little black lab-shepherd mix you ever saw. Harper adored Kinsey; they frisked like two puppies.

I liked having Harper around. I didn't let her have her cell phone at the table, and that ticked her off, but sometimes, in the late afternoon before Leah got home, we baked cookies, and she gave me grief about how awful they were without gluten or butter, and then she scoffed about a dozen while telling me about her latest crush. Man, I wish I could eat like that. She had shot up like a weed that year; it was like she couldn't feed the engine of her body fast enough. She was a lot like her father, rangy and blond. No wonder her phone teemed with messages.

One time, she was working on a report for school, about abortion rights. Why do they give these impossible topics to kids? We were sitting in the front room with some cookies, looking out across the street towards the little house she shared with her mother. "I'm pro-life," she declared.

I said, "You know that's just rhetoric, right? They call it 'pro-life' just so it makes their opponents sound like they're anti-life, or pro-death."

She made an impatient face, with Mac's cheekbones. I went on.

"Pro-choice people care about the *quality* of life. They want to protect women who aren't ready to have children. Women who want to have control over their own bodies."

"They should have thought about that before they got knocked up," she said. God, was I ever that sure of my rightness?

I changed the subject. I didn't think it was my place to be preaching to my neighbor's daughter. Besides, I didn't want Harper to feel unwelcome in our house just because we disagreed on some things.

Before long, though, she stopped coming over. I asked Ruth about it, tentatively, and she said, "Oh, it's that boy."

"What boy?"

"Josh," she said. "Like his name itself is a joke."

"But she's serious about him?"

"Serious," she said, "What's serious? We're talking about a hank of hair with a penis."

After that, we just saw Harper in passing, busting out of the house on her way to this or that. She was off to the races.

For a few days it seemed like the bus had just been abandoned—but then we woke up to discover that it wasn't in front of Ruth's house anymore; it had migrated down a few doors, and was now in front of the Marriotts'. Bud Marriott was furious. He stopped his lawnmower when I walked by with Kinsey, just to tell me. He said he had called the cops, complaining that the thing was a nuisance; he couldn't see around it when he was backing out of his driveway, it was damn dangerous. The cops said they couldn't do anything; it was perfectly legal to park a private vehicle on the street. "But there's a catch," Bud said. "You can't leave it in the same place more than three days at a time. That's vagrancy." Well, whoever was in charge of the bus apparently knew this, too. You could almost see the steam coming out of Bud's ears. When I didn't say anything else, he yanked extra hard on the lawnmower starter. But two days later the bus moved on down to a spot in front of the Graeberts', and he calmed down.

On Front Porch Forum there were all sorts of opinions and theories. You know, it's useful to have that website, you learn about the yard sales and the missing cats—but some people have too much time on their hands. Someone said the bus must be related to the construction of the new parkway, a few blocks away; maybe it would carry workers to and from the site. But why would it be parked here already? Empty? The parkway was still in the appeal process, because lots of people didn't want it to bring more traffic so close to our neighborhood. Leah was working against it through official channels, lobbying the mayor's office, organizing meetings to raise awareness. She said there was no evidence that the bus was connected to the construction; that was just paranoia. But what else is Front Porch Forum for?

Somebody else suggested that it could be a mobile hangout for a bunch of hippies, like those Island Pond people who came to town about twenty years ago. That would explain the sloppy paint job, and it was true that we had been seeing more stringy-haired kids in the park recently. When I walked Kinsey in the morning, I found the remains of little campfires, sometimes with empty bottles and used condoms. It was gross. Leah said the park was a public space, you've got to expect a used condom or two. "At least they're practicing safe sex," she said.

But if it was hippies, wouldn't they have festooned the bus with brighter paint, and dried flowers, or something? Wouldn't there be guys hanging around playing guitars? Hippies aren't exactly famous for discretion. Why didn't we see them on the bus itself? Why didn't we ever see *anyone* on the bus? And how the hell did it move every three days?

There was one thread on the forum suggesting that the bus had been landed by aliens who were controlling it remotely. It was an advance scouting mission. Right. Like aliens would land in the South End of Burlington, Vermont. On our block. What would they be scouting for here? Somebody said that of course they'd reconnoiter in an inconspicuous place; they didn't want to draw attention. If pets and children started disappearing, then we'd know. But I'm pretty sure that whole thread was just a put-on; the subject heading was "Unidentified Parked Object."

The summer advanced. Because of my own health issues, I was working part-time at the bookstore, and that was fine with Marion, my boss. Summer's a slow time for books, and she was glad to cut back on wages for a while. She wasn't nuts about my approach to bookselling, anyway. All five of us on the staff shared responsibility for our stock; the idea was that we pooled our collective knowledge of what the community wanted to read. The trouble was, I kept ordering poetry. Marion said that if we were going to compete with Amazon, every inch of shelf space in that little shop had to justify itself. Books that didn't sell in two weeks were to be sent back to the distributor, and of course we had to pay for the shipping, so if we ordered unwisely we not only wasted shelf space on something unprofitable but we paid for it coming and going. But customers need time to be won over to poetry, and when the time comes, they need to know that you've got some. So maybe sometimes I overlooked the fact that certain collections of poems had been sitting unsold for months. Who were we kidding, anyway? There was no way we could compete with Amazon. Bookstores are community centers that happen to be decorated with books. Might as well have good ones. Above the literature section, I put up a nice little hand-lettered sign:

> It is difficult
> to get the news from poems
> but men die miserably every day
> for lack
> of what is found there.

"Women too," somebody scribbled in ballpoint.

Once in a while Marion noticed that the store was flush with contemporary poets, the ones who really don't sell — Delanty, Engels, Howe, Huddle, Purpura, Shockley. She gave me The Look, and I started packing up boxes to send back to the publishers.

Back in the neighborhood, the community garden flourished. Ruth had been instrumental in organizing it, just a few years before. She taught Environmental Studies at the college, and said that if every neighborhood had its own garden, cultivated for its own needs and climate, we could change the whole corrupt food infrastructure. Under her guidance, a bunch of the neighbors took a grassy patch of hillside and turned it into a ragged but thriving haven for veggies and flowers. Mac helped put up the wire fence around it, and Harper held the sledge with him for the cameras as they drove the last stakes for the gate. She must have been ten at the time, a little tow-headed rapscallion, always underfoot or up on her daddy's shoulders. I don't know why they didn't have another child, but I guess it was for the best.

In the summer of the bus, Ruth spent a lot of time in that garden. We'd had a ton of rain that spring, which was a drag at the time, but by late July the tomatoes and zucchini were going crazy. Ruth had planted a border of sunflowers all around her plot—just for fun, she said— and the sunflowers sprang up like soldiers. She had to cut down a few stalks just to create a doorway, so she could get in there to water and weed. When the grackles started picking on the sunflowers, she sank a stake in the ground and nailed another stake across the top to make a T, then hung one of Mac's old flannel shirts on it. Amazingly, the grackles backed off. I don't know where she got the energy.

Leah and I didn't go for a share in the garden, because we were busy enough with our own flower plots in the front yard. Getting your hands in the dirt is really satisfying, especially if it's the good dark loamy stuff. We had a truckload of it brought in, because we were so close to the lake that the ground tended to be solid unplantable clay. I did most of the tending, because Leah was so busy at work, embroiled in the fight against the parkway.

Like most of the boomers in the neighborhood, Ruth was against the parkway, but she thought Leah's work was a waste of time. "You can't work within the system," she said. "The system is rotten through and through. You've got to take direct action." This was the kind of Old Lefty talk that made Harper roll her eyes.

The older generation tended to favor the parkway. Some of them liked to stop and chat as I worked in our front garden. Elly Taylor stood at the curb and said, "Alvin always said that if you get in the way of progress, it will just bulldoze you down. People want to drive into town! Pine Street is a mess! If we don't improve access, downtown will collapse. All those little businesses will go belly up." She didn't mention the bookstore by name.

Standing beside her, Bud Marriott added, "And when that happens, our property values will sink out of sight."

After they left, I caught a whiff of something familiar. Joe Palawczuk's aftershave: you could always smell him coming. He didn't say much, just stood there in his white t-shirt, suspenders holding his old gray work trousers up to his big comfortable gut. I don't think he was thrilled to have a pair of middle-aged women owning a house on the street, with no kids—it just wasn't the South End he grew up in. But he just said, "Nice work, nice work! The whatsits are really coming along, aren't they?" And he pointed at the bee balm. He was right, it was going gangbusters.

I walked to the park with Kinsey a couple of times a day, and I always made a point of checking on Ruth's garden plot. You had to lean in beyond the screen of sunflowers to see into that little room, and often she was there, on her knees in the dirt, as if she was praying. When she was in the garden, she didn't talk much. She had an iPod clamped to her arm, and ear buds tucked in under her head wrap; her head bobbed to the beat, and sometimes if she didn't see you she'd be singing a scrap of a lyric, too loud. She used to have a rich, plummy contralto, but her voice had become croaky thanks to the radiation. When she looked up and pulled out the ear buds, I asked what she was listening to, and she said Anais Mitchell's recording of the Child Ballads. I nodded like I knew what she was talking about, and she plugged the ear buds back in and returned to her weeding. As Kinsey pulled me away, I heard her croak, "Nobody let him in!"

When I got home I spent some time with Anais Mitchell on YouTube, and man, those ballads were awful. I mean, the singing was good, and the harmonies were sweet — but the stories! They were all tales of fateful love — fathers who insisted that their daughters marry money, mothers who cursed their sons for leaving home, children who did what they had to do anyway. In "Clyde Water," one of those doomed sons sets out to meet his sweet forbidden Margaret knowing full well that he'll probably never come home. "Make me a wreck as I come back," he cries, "spare me as I'm goin'." It was terrible. I listened to it over and over.

Meanwhile, the bus kept moving up and down the street, and it continued to be a popular topic of conversation for garden-gawkers who stopped by our front yard. One morning Elly Taylor said she had seen somebody leaving it the night before, and I couldn't help saying, "From your top-floor room?" She said no, from her front porch, when she got up in the middle of the night for a little hot milk. I wondered how anyone could want hot milk on a sticky August night. I knew she had never got air conditioning, because she told us all the time how oppressive the heat was in her little house. She said a hot drink was the way to cool off—something crazy about how the heat inside your body makes your skin cooler. Anyway, she took her cup of hot milk out on her porch, and just then, she said, she saw a man in a big hat step off the bus and walk down the street toward the park.

"A big hat?" I said.

"A big straw hat. A floppy sun hat, like you'd wear at the beach."

"How do you know it was a man? Did he say anything?"

"Oh no, he didn't see me. I stayed on the porch, in the dark. But I could just tell it was a man. He was tall."

"What was he wearing?"

"A white shirt. Dark trousers. Like one of those Jehovah's people who go door to door."

"And he just walked down the street."

"Right down the middle. He didn't use the sidewalk. Course, there was no traffic at that hour, so he could."

"Did you call the cops?"

"No!" She looked like I had insulted her intelligence. "What would I tell the police? That someone got out of a private vehicle and walked down the street? As if that was against the law?"

I guessed she had a point there, so I turned back to deadheading the marigolds. I was accumulating a nice handful of dry petals in my left hand, squeezing so as to compact them and make room for more. Elly gave me a funny look; I guess she was hoping I'd ask her for more non-information on the Floppy Hat Man. But I didn't have anything else to ask, and eventually she sighed and moved on.

When Joe Palawczuk stopped by a little later, I asked him if he had heard anything new about the bus, and he said, "You mean about the man in the flowing white robe?"

"There was a man in a flowing white robe?"

"That's what Bud Marriott says."

"Did he see this man?" I stood up from my weeding crouch. My knees can't take it too long at one time.

"No, I don't think so." Joe looked up into the silver maple above us. His memory could be a little fuzzy; sometimes he looked away in order to recollect what he was saying. "No," he said finally. "Somebody told him."

"Was it Elly Taylor?"

"Yes." He looked down the street toward the park, two hundred yards away. "No. Maybe."

Then he looked back at the garden. "The geraniums

are looking good," he said, and walked off towards his house. I thanked him. We didn't have any geraniums.

A little later, I walked Kinsey down to the park. It was still early; the fields and tennis courts were empty. You might have thought Kinsey would tire of the park, where she was brought to do her business at least twice a day. But nothing made her happier than that big open space with its carnival of scents. I walked her past the swing set and that collection of plastic tubes and chutes and poles for climbing and sliding and breaking bones. The city hadn't provided any fresh wood chips for a couple of years now, and the ground underneath it was a slab of hard clay. We walked to the spindly little tree by the baseball field, with its plaque in memory of the Graeberts' boy Hudson, who died in a swimming accident the year before. He had been a star on that field. That morning I cried, I don't know why. I didn't let Kinsey pee there.

Even as we approached the community garden, something didn't look right. Usually you'd see Mac's red flannel shirt from a distance, like a banner on the ramparts. On that morning after Elly Taylor's sighting of the Man in the Floppy Hat—or the Man in the Mormon Suit, or whatever he was—there was no shirt. The two stakes were charred black, and as we got closer I saw ashy shreds of red flannel in the grass. I leaned in past the sunflowers, and peered into Ruth's plot.

It was a mess. It had been trampled and flattened by something. Or someone. Zucchini that Ruth had tended so carefully all summer, kale and tomatoes and spinach—

all of it was smashed and scrambled, as if someone had decided to make a big pot of ratatouille. Kinsey sniffed at it briefly and backed away. I just stood there and stared.

I sleepwalked around the store that afternoon, checking inventory, and ordered a whole slew of poetry. In the evening I took Ruth some mac 'n' cheese. She didn't invite me in. Standing at the door in a pale blue housecoat and a matching headwrap, she looked like a nineteenth-century painting of The Lady at Home. Her dark blue eyes had always been her best feature; now, with her pink chemo complexion, they popped even more. I held the dish out to her, and she looked down at it like it was a foreign object, which I guess it was: under the aluminum foil, it could have been anything, brownies or wingnuts. I handed it to her, and asked her about the garden.

She said, "You know, people like destroying things." She paused. "Remember when you were a kid, in the winter, and you saw a puddle covered with ice? What was the first thing you wanted to do?"

"Smash it!" I said. We both laughed.

"I couldn't have eaten any of those vegetables, anyway," she said. "Way too much roughage for my tender system." She patted her substantial midsection, and smiled.

"Ruth," I said, and then I didn't know what else to say. I must have done something with my hands.

"I just don't want to linger," she said. "You know?"

I didn't know. She was like the person in a fairy tale who stops you and demands that you answer a riddle. But I nodded. A car went by behind me. "I should get home for dinner," I said. "You know how cranky Leah gets when I'm late."

She smiled again. Anyone who looked could see that Leah's car wasn't home yet. Ruth thanked me again and closed the door.

Elly Taylor said it had to be Mac who trampled Ruth's garden. "I told her," she said as she stood by our garden the next day, "I told her it wasn't a good idea to use one of his old shirts for a scarecrow. It was like waving a red flag at a bull! You know he's still got a thing for her."

"Strange way to show it," I said, flicking a Japanese beetle off a poppy. We had a bad infestation of beetles that year, and they had a thing for poppies. There was nothing you could use on them without killing the flowers, too.

Elly said, "Oh, you know how juvenile people can be."

I nodded. If Mac was around, why hadn't anyone seen him in a year and a half? I think it drove Elly crazy not to know more about Ruth's business. Ruth didn't "share." Maybe Elly saw me on Ruth's stoop, and hoped I would spill. I didn't say anything. Sometimes you just had to let Elly run out of gas, and she walked away of her own accord.

I wasn't sleeping much that summer. For some reason I just didn't want to go to bed at night; I wanted to stay up as long as possible. Leah and I always watched the nightly news, which wasn't exactly conducive to sleep. Terrorists seemed to be everywhere, refugees were pouring into Europe, white cops were shooting black boys in our cities. Leah always went to bed by 11:30, so she could be up and off to work by 8. She gave Kinsey the first morning walk, and often she left me a little note about the day to come. "Soy milk," it might say, or "Dinner at Faith and Laura's."

I just stayed up later and later. I sat in the front room and watched old episodes of "The Voice" that I'd DVRed; I read Sue Grafton mysteries, working my way through the alphabet; I did word puzzles in old copies of the Sunday paper that we saved for just that purpose. As traffic thinned, the street got quieter and quieter. By 2 AM the only thing you'd hear would be the moan of a freight train down by the lake.

As we moved into September, there was less and less talk about the bus. It kept moving every few days, and occasionally someone would be freshly annoyed to find it looming at their own curb, but there didn't seem to be anything we could do about it. It's amazing how people get used to things. Front Porch Forum reverted to chatter about the parkway, which seemed to be moving ahead again. Leah got even busier in the campaign to stop it. There was going to be an open hearing soon, and she wanted to be ready.

It must have been strange for Ruth to be home that September, for the first time since childhood, as everyone else was going back to school. Everyone except Harper, that is. I mean, she was still *in* school, technically, but that didn't mean she was *at* school. One day I got a phone call from the principal's office—a robo-call, reporting that "your student" was not present in home room that morning. That was weird; Leah and I didn't have a "student." When I called them back, the administrative assistant said ours was the number Harper Milliband provided. That school was a mess.

When I called Ruth, she didn't sound surprised. "I've done everything I can," she said. "I forbade her to see that boy—as if I could make it stop. I cut off her allowance, and she just nodded, like 'Mom, you think this is about money?' I took away her cell phone—and then I couldn't call her anymore. I told her she'd be grounded if I got any more of those absence calls from the high school—and she gives them your number instead. I guess she thought you wouldn't narc on her."

I winced. "So now she's grounded?"

"Oh, she's grounded as hell. If I can find her to let her know." She laughed. How could she laugh? I laughed, too.

By the end of September, the big ginkgo in the Marriotts' yard had gone completely gold. Year after year, that damn tree broke my heart. It was a spectacular blaze, almost too gorgeous to look at. And of course it just signified one thing. Days growing shorter, nights coming sooner, the ridiculous cold at the door. I couldn't bear it. For a few days I had one of my rough patches, in which I just couldn't get out of the house. I was so tired it made me dizzy just to get out of bed. The hot flashes had started that summer, too—a sudden prickly heat that made me anxious, like my whole body had restless leg syndrome.

What a lovely way for nature to tell you that the one thing you were engineered for is now officially over. When I did get up, I just wanted to eat all day. I mean, I was ravenous. I stood at the open refrigerator and stared at all the food that would make me sick. Then I ate some more gluten-free crackers.

Marion cut me some slack at work. Probably she would take the opportunity to clear all the poetry off the shelves. And Leah was great, as usual; she walked Kinsey twice a day, and got the groceries, and checked on me when she came home. I was using the downstairs bedroom, so I wouldn't bother her with my weird schedule.

But she wasn't much of a news source. When I asked her about the bus, she made a blank face.

"The bus!" I said, rolling my eyes. "You know: dark, hulking thing parked on the street? Moving mysteriously up and down the block? The Man in the Floppy Hat?"

She brightened. "Oh," she said, "I don't know. I haven't seen it for days. Maybe it belonged to some school, after all."

I sighed.

Leah said, "I'm not good at this, am I?"

The first day I felt well enough, I took Kinsey out for a walk, and of course there it was, parked at the curb, right where our block dead-ended into the park. You could hardly see it down there, out of the way, bothering no one. But somehow it still creeped me out.

On the way home, I stopped at Ruth's. It took her a long time to answer the door; I almost gave up on her. But then there she was, and she looked strange—extra pale, and bloated, like she was retaining water. Maybe it was because she wasn't getting out to the garden anymore. Or maybe it was just where she was in the chemo cycle. But her eyes, her deep blue eyes, looked more intense than ever. Or maybe it's just in retrospect that I say this.

Again, she didn't invite me in, and I didn't blame her; she looked too tired for company. I asked if she had noticed that the bus had moved down to the park.

She nodded, and said, "Did you know that you can just walk onto it?"

"Walk onto it?"

"Yeah. You know, it's one of those old-style school buses, with the folding door. You just push in the middle, and it gives."

"So—did you?"

"Yep. And you know what I found?"

"What?"

"The windows were closed, so the whole thing stank of pot and unwashed clothes." She smiled. "In the back, they had taken out three rows of seats; you could see where the bolts were removed from the floor. In that open space there was a big old mattress—and that was about it. An ashtray, some trash. They had cleared out pretty thoroughly."

"They?"

"Harper and Josh."

"How do you know?"

"That mattress had been in our basement for years. I

don't know why Mac wanted to hold onto that old thing. It was mildewed and stained; in the summer you could smell it as soon as you opened the basement door. Well, at least they got it out of the house."

"And where are they now?"

"Beats the hell out of me. I hope they've got something to sleep on."

She laughed, and shut the door.

I walked Kinsey down there, but she didn't want anything to do with the bus. I can't say I blamed her.

When the explosion ripped into the night, I was already awake. I had just taken a bath — another little night-time routine — and had my hair wrapped up in a white towel. That slowed me down when it came to getting outside; I didn't want to go out in the cool fall air with wet hair. By the time I had blow-dried it and combed it out, Leah's pale face was at the bathroom door.

"What the hell was that?"

"An explosion, out on the street."

"What are you doing?"

"Fixing my hair."

"For God's sake," she said. I followed her to the mudroom, where we threw on coats over our bathrobes.

We didn't need the coats: it was a mild night. The Graeberts were coming out of their front door; Bud and Sally Marriott were barely visible ahead of us, walking toward the park. We followed them. You could already smell the acrid fumes of gasoline.

Down at the end of the block, the flames were like a beacon drawing us all out of our homes. From a distance it was an indistinct ball of fire, like something out of an action movie. As we got closer, we could tell: it was the bus.

Elly Taylor was already there, of course; she hadn't bothered putting a coat over her pink floral bathrobe. So was Joe Palawczuk, in his white tee shirt and suspenders—did he sleep like that? Nobody seemed to know what to do. Bud said to Sally, "I should go back for the fire extinguisher," but he didn't do anything. It was like a bonfire; we all just watched. Who knew that a thing made of metal and glass could burn like that? For a minute I worried about the poplars above it, lining the edge of the park: what if they caught fire, too? But then the fire truck arrived, and they hosed it down, with a lot of whoosh and bustle, and when the flames had been doused, it was possible to see, under the streetlight, in the charred shell of the bus, strapped into the driver's seat, a body. All I could think, at the time, was why hadn't there been screams?

Leah and I got the job of cleaning out Ruth's house. She was an only child, and her parents were long gone. And Mac? We couldn't find him. He wasn't a Facebook kind of guy. I can't say we tried very hard.

There wasn't a lot of cleaning to do, anyway. Everything was in impeccable order. With the exception of a small assortment of clothes in the bedroom, the closets were empty. The bookcases that lined her study and living room were bare, and dusted; we found books in boxes, labeled with the names of the friends who should receive them. One of the boxes was for us. Even the refrigerator was virtually empty, and well scrubbed. We didn't find a note. The whole house was a note.

Apparently you can rig up a timer that will set off an explosive whenever you want it to blow. You can learn it from a dozen sites on the web.

They got the body out right away, of course, although it was far too late. But the black shell of the bus sat there for a few days. Maybe they didn't know what to do with it. When the tow truck finally came, several of us stood to watch as the garage guys loaded the thing and hauled it away. They used a big push broom to sweep the space by the curb, but there were still bits of broken glass and scraps of unidentifiable char—flakes of burnt paint, maybe.

And Harper? Harper was gone as Amelia Earhart. We got robo-calls from the high school for weeks. Our student wasn't in homeroom. Leah finally called them and told them to desist.

It's been six months now, and the gingko is totally bare. I'm back in the bookstore, which is still hanging on, in spite of the unsold poetry. A new family has moved in across the street, a couple with two young kids. I took them some cookies, with regular flour and loads of butter. Elly Taylor says the kids are both on medication for ADHD. Sometimes Kinsey and I walk over to the community garden, and I look into Ruth's old plot, which is covered in snow. I make mental plans to plant things— sweet alyssum and lavender, lambs ear, trillium. Maybe I will. They still haven't built the parkway. Yet.

OH! YOU PRETTY THINGS

When you blew up the bus, I was just ten miles away. But you understood, didn't you? I just couldn't be there. I just couldn't. I had been there and been there and been there, and I had burned my patience to the socket. How was I supposed to know you would strap yourself into that bus and blow it all up?

The bus had been a magic place for me. Josh loved it so much, and I came to love it, too. He had bought it—or "borrowed" it, I don't know—and done so much work on it. Mr. Marriott asked me once, "Harper, do you know anything about the bus?" That dark hulking thing that was parked on our street all last summer? Even at half the length of a typical school bus, it was imposing, and I guess it was unsightly for our street, where all the houses were so well behaved, standing at attention behind their little lawns. A mini school bus, painted a dirty matte green, windows veiled with curtains inside, wasn't the kind of thing you'd expect to find parked on Louise Street. And that's why we parked it there. Josh said that if we moved it every three days, they couldn't get us for vagrancy. There's no law that says you can't sleep in a legally parked vehicle. Mr. Marriott was steamed. I just shrugged and asked him how little Sally was doing. People can't resist talking about the grandkids.

Josh was so proud of that bus. He had removed the rear seats on both sides, making plenty of room for a mattress and a little pot-bellied stove, with a pipe that went up through a well-caulked hole in the roof. "It's got everything we need," he said when he first showed it to me that spring, in the parking lot behind T. J. Maxx.

"We?" I asked. "What are we going to do with it? Sell chili dogs from the emergency door?"

"No," he said, looking hurt. He shook the long brown hair from his eyes, and squared up his bony shoulders. "We're going to live in it."

And that was how he got me. He seduced me by having a big idea, and then by planting me in it.

I loved that bus. It was fun to take it out on the road, riding high above traffic, getting funny looks from people who didn't expect the driver to be a longhaired dude in a knit cap, with a tall blonde girl riding right behind him. And at night it was cozy in the back, with the curtains drawn and the windows open, crickets singing on the breeze.

So when you blew it up, well, let's just say I had feelings.

Did you ever have something like that? A place where you could go to escape Nana and Poppy? You never talked about stuff like that—maybe you didn't want to give me ideas. I always had trouble imagining that you had ever been a teenager. I pictured you doing things like Model U.N. and Save The Earth, organizing and mobilizing the Good Kids to Make a Difference. It must have been hard for you when I didn't want to be mobilized. We Shall Not Be Moved, that was my theme song.

Still, when Dad came along there must have been some stirrings in Ruth World, right? Dad may have been an underachiever, but he was a man of the flesh. You never talked about that, either. After he left, you didn't talk about him at all. Dad was like one of those opposition figures who go missing in South America; he was The Disappeared. And I guess I can't blame you: when Josh took off, I felt like cut meat walking. Still, it probably would have been good if I could have imagined you as a giddy teenager, or even a brokenhearted one. If I had ever seen you cry.

But you didn't do giddy. Or tears. I guess you wanted to be strong for me. Funny how I would have felt better if you could have been weak, like me.

When Dad left, you doubled down. You had to be both mother and father, planner and watcher, breadwinner, cook, and chief bottle-washer. And of course you had your job to mind—your precious students, your writing, and the activism it was all founded on. You can't have slept much in those years. I remember getting up, one night when I couldn't sleep, and finding you at the kitchen table, under the old hanging light, so intent on your papers you didn't even hear me. And I wasn't impressed. I just wanted to watch "The Gilmore Girls" with you, or walk a dog in the park. When Dad took Sloppy Joe with him, I was crushed — it was almost worse than losing Dad. But Sloppy was always more Dad's than yours. You didn't have time for a dog.

What was I supposed to do, Mom? When Josh came along, I just wanted out.

I know you never liked him. You thought he was "ill bred," because he didn't take off his hat in the house. You couldn't get him to talk about politics — and in your book a young person who didn't care about GMOs or climate change was just a waste of space. Josh wasn't like that, OK? Not everybody has to be the righteous protester. We didn't grow up with Dylan, like you. We thought Dylan was a gnarly old guy who sounded like the sixties on life support. But we did have our own protest movement: parking the bus in our quiet little neighborhood, and living in it all that summer. We called it Occupy Louise Street.

So you were right about Josh. He was ill bred, and too old for me; he was just looking for sex and adventure. His only ambition was to have no ambition. But it didn't seem to occur to you that being right didn't help your cause. It just made me want to go further wrong. I wanted sex and adventure, too. And if you disapproved, well, that was just gravy.

When I shaved my head, I thought of Rapunzel. You used to read to me from that fairy tale book because it was "part of our cultural heritage," even though you always had to point out all the politically unacceptable parts. You wanted to keep me locked in a tower; I didn't want to give you any rope. Josh liked running his hand over my fuzz.

Is it worse being an only child or the mother of an only child? People used to look at me sadly. So much pressure, they said. No siblings to play with, to blaze trails, to distract the parents from your own missteps. But I wondered, even then, if it was worse for you. There was no replacement child, no insurance policy. You put all your chips on one number. And then Dad left.

I remember so many things about him—but I know you wouldn't want to hear them. You'd tell me I'm romanticizing, just because he was gone. I guess I don't blame you. But still, I'm allowed to remember, especially now. I remember his study, where sometimes he let me watch stuff on his computer, even though I was supposed to be a "screen-free" kid. In my memory, that room smells like Cheez Doodles, which he pulled out of his desk drawer, precious contraband in a house with no junk food. He made sure that before we went back into Ruth World I washed that salty orange stain from my hands. It was weird going in there later, that guest room that never had guests.

I remember the volleyball games in the back yard with his friends from the library, those summer afternoons, barefoot in the grass, Van Morrison on the boombox, lemonade for me and cheap beer for everyone else. He said it had to be Pabst; he would not have snooty microbrews at his parties. He always had me play in the middle, because I was good at digs; I was "the barrow," he said. I liked that word. One time, when I got all upset about flubbing a shot, he said, "Harpo, you're trying too hard. Trying too hard is rock and roll kryptonite."

I remember him playing piano, badly, the old upright that you moved to the basement when I quit those awful lessons. Sometimes I sat on his lap while he pounded out songs from Bowie's "Hunky Dory"—"the most underrated album ever," he said. He made me believe, for a while, that you and he were just a couple of kooks.

He loved all his stupid sports so much. Fancy Baseball in the summer, Fancy Football fall and winter. This time of year, he would be deep in his precious brackets. He called in sick on those days in March—did you know? He always waited until you left for work, and told me not to tell. God knows how many pools he was in. I'd come home from school and find him agonizing over the Cleveland State Zephyrs or somebody, praying for some oversized boy to make a free throw. I know it made you crazy. All that hype, all those beer commercials, all that energy misspent on a bunch of tall young men in shorts. But I don't think I ever saw Dad happier. And I could imagine that if once upon a time he'd lavished that kind of passion on you, well, no wonder you fell for him.

It must have been infuriating, after Dad left, when I spent so much time in my room, door closed like a giant hand. But I didn't feel like talking. I just wanted to listen to my music, Justin Bieber and the cute boy bands I loved then, all those songs about lost teenage love. Oh, and I wanted to eat all the time, just like I do now — those snacks I picked up at Cumby's on the way home from school and smuggled into the house. When you found the Little Debbie wrappers and started searching my backpack, I stuffed things under my sweater, into my armpits, and walked stiff-armed into the house and up the stairs, so I could eat them in my room. There's nothing like a Devil Dog warmed to body temperature.

But it cut both ways, that silence in our house. There were plenty of things you never told me — like why Dad left, and why you had ever said yes to him in the first place, and how you felt about it all. I had to intuit things, and learn them from Evie, who was not exactly an unbiased source. "Fuckin' Mac," she said, that year when you got sick and I spent so many afternoons in their big kitchen across the street. "You'd think maybe he would come help out with his daughter if he heard that her mother was sick. But not our Mac — he had to be free. Who knew freedom could be so destructive?"

I never knew if Dad even heard about your illness. He had cleared out two years before, leaving our little college town for parts unknown. He must have had projects. He was always going to write, he said — like, books. But his job in the university library, cataloguing all the books by other people, was just a constant reminder that his own book wasn't happening, that he had to "clear the decks" to make it possible. "All right," Evie said, "so clear the fuckin' decks. Quit your job if you have to. But leave your thirteen-year-old daughter who adores you without a word? What kind of bastard does that?" If he didn't know that you had cancer, Evie said, that was no better than if he knew and was deliberately staying away. You need to know things about the mother of your child.

Leah gave Evie hard looks when she bad-mouthed Dad in front of me. But Evie didn't care. When she got wound up there was no stopping her. And Leah wasn't there a lot of the time: she was caught up in the Community Action work, lobbying for affordable housing, fighting against the parkway that would come too close to our little neighborhood. So a lot of the time that year, it was just me and Evie at their kitchen table, with gluten-free cookies fresh from the oven and The Mix 101 on the radio. This was a compromise somewhere between Evie's Adele and my Maroon 5. We both thought it was too close to the other's preference.

Evie was the one who told me the epic story of my birth—the 28-hour labor, with the midwife trying everything to induce it, but no drugs, you insisted, you wanted to experience it all, and Dad tearing his hair out—so that's where it went—and saying, "Honey, let's go to the hospital," but no, it had to be a home birth, and Evie and Leah coming over after work, reading you poetry, holding your hand, and finally, at 3 AM, you were screaming and sweating—of course it was July, and of course we didn't have AC, not in your all-natural house—crouching in the kitchen because you just couldn't stay in bed, and of course I got stuck, and in the effort to get out I acquired my first broken nose. Was that why you didn't tell me that story? For years I hated my nose, and tried to cover it up when I had to speak in school, which wasn't exactly easy: try covering your nose while talking. I wanted to get it fixed—but of course you wouldn't go for that, that would have been unnatural. Dad said it made me "distinctive." Nice try, Dad. Eventually, though, I came to like it. Dad was right. Josh used to trace it with a finger when we lay together on the mattress in the back of the bus.

But you should have just taken the drugs, Mom. I sure will.

So: we didn't tell each other much. I never told you, for instance, what that weirdo shrink suggested when I was having so much trouble at school. Anyone else would have just put me on Adderall like the other kids, but not Dr. Finst. He clapped his hands together like he was sitting down to a Thanksgiving turkey, and he said, "So, do you masturbate?" You could've knocked me down with a feather. I fumbled out some kind of totally dishonest no, and he said, "Well, you should. Orgasm releases oxytocin and lowers cortisol." I looked those words up as soon as I got back to the school computer. And you know, he was right? Whatever got released or lowered, I started feeling better. So I took my medicine. Later, Josh became my hand. He conjured me.

By then, you and I were doing the home-schooling thing again, because you had another sabbatical. Some professors get a sabbatical and take off to study ruins in Mexico or archives in Italy — I know, because I talked to the other PKs. But not Mother Gothel. No, you said, ""Hmm, I think I'll stay home and torture my daughter." The first time, back when I was in third grade, it was OK, because Dad was still around and you were mostly happy, and I didn't know any better. I mean, I thought it was weird that we spent so much time on the 2004 tsunami — none of the kids at the park were doing that. But you said it was a perfect way to cover science (plate tectonics and climate change) and social science (how the people who lived in the most dangerous zones are always the poor people, and how little help they got from their govern- ments) and multicultural awareness — I knew more about Pacific Islanders than anyone at the jungle gym. I was pretty pleased with myself. And I was also freaked out. What kind of God allows such things to happen? I'm not sure that was part of the lesson plan. But maybe it was. You wanted me to know the world, and I have to admit I learned a lot.

By the time of the next sabbatical, though, it was just misery. You were the seven-year bitch. I know you wanted to reconnect after Dad left. And you were right that the high school might not be the best place for a kid who was itching to try some controlled substances. But really, Mom? Did it really seem wise to keep me home all the time when you and I could barely stand each other's smell? Isn't the whole point of school that it gives kids a way to get out of the house? I know, it probably wasn't the best learning strategy when I just clapped my hands over my ears and went Na na na na na na na.

Still, I got to read Emily Dickinson. I have to thank you for that. I loved those funky dashes of hers.

> I cannot meet the Spring unmoved —
> I feel the old desire —
> A Hurry, with a lingering, mixed,
> A Warrant to be fair —

We also studied the Old Testament, because you wanted me to know my Jewish heritage. I was less crazy about that, because of all the family mishegas. It just looked so much easier to be a lapsed Presbyterian, like Dad. Still, don't worry, I got all the stuff about the Exodus, and escape from bondage, and all that. I'll be thinking of it soon, at Passover.

In fact, the first time I got drunk was at a seder. Yes, Manischewitz was the vehicle, and I drove it as hard as I could. Dad used to say "Man oh manischewitz," with a smile and a sigh, and then cross himself just to enrich the cultural confusion. I didn't know that stuff was supposed to be so bad. How can you know when you've had no wine before? I only knew that I was starved after the fasting — I was the firstborn child, after all — and the table was loaded with all that inedible stuff — gefilte fish and that cardboard matzo, squash soufflé and the sourest pickles ever, and we had to wait forever for the brisket and the haroseth while you and others were reading unintelligible scripture passages — but here was this great sweet purple drink, like Welch's with a wicked kick, and Cousin Hermie, who I only ever saw at seders, kept filling my glass with a grin, and you were reading aloud and bustling back and forth to the kitchen and looking out for all the guests, all those "Passover Orphans" from the university reclining on the floor around the big makeshift table in the living room, so you didn't have the usual hawk eye on me, and man oh manischewitz, I guzzled it down, and then splattered it all over the front hall toilet. Couldn't even make it upstairs for some privacy. We hadn't even got to the Four Questions yet. What makes this night different from all other nights? Harper is ralphing down the hall.

I must have been twelve at the time, because Dad was still there. He came and crouched beside me, put his hand on my back and said, "It's OK, kid." He always called me kid, and I confess I kind of liked it, even though I wouldn't have let you call me that for anything. Not that you would have considered it, anyway: you didn't go for nicknames, so I was always Harper to you, or even Harper Mackenzie, the Jewish-Scottish hope of the Milliband-Morgan family. "Kid" was so much simpler.

And I was a kid, even though I was already five-foot-nine and my boobs were well on the way. Maybe that was why Cousin Hermie was grinning. You kept telling me that I had to find my own "best self," and that sounded like a good thing, but I had no idea what it was. At school, my best self was not good enough for gold stars, or to get invited to Francie Lampson's sleepovers. What you really wanted was for me to be a version of your self at that age — brainy, independent, smarter than all the boys in your class, not to mention the girls. After Dad left, I pretty much gave up on all that. What if my own best self was just what I was, a tall kid with a crooked nose who would rather be hanging out with the stoner boys in the park?

And then you got sick. Was there a cause and effect, Mom? I tried the hypotheses. 1. Dad leaves; Mom gets sick. But you didn't get sick until two years later. What's the expiration date on grief? 2. Dad leaves, Harper goes rogue, Mom gets sick. This one made more sense. How could I test it? Go even roguer. If Mom gets sicker, that might look like proof. 3. It's all random, just a tangle of cells that invade when they fucking feel like it, like a thirty-foot wall of water that drops out of the sky and crushes a whole island. No, that one was inconceivable.

"Inconceivable!" said Vizzini the Sicilian in "The Princess Bride." I loved that movie so much. Of course, every inconceivable thing turned out to be perfectly conceivable.

I should have been able to bear it. I was the daughter of Ruth Milliband, beloved professor, community organizer, unstoppable force for good. But I wasn't you, Mom. I felt completely stoppable.

You said you were fine — which I knew was a total lie. You lost your hair, your skin went ashy, you put on even more weight, and you joked about it like a brave survivor. You were the chemo sapien, you were the cancer schlepper. I should have been able to laugh. I should have known how much pain you were in.

You said I should focus on school. You suggested I spend more time at Evie and Leah's, because I shouldn't have to live in the Krankenhaus. Ruth being clever again.

So I did, for a while. Evie and Leah were great. I would go over there straight from school, and hang out with Evie in their kitchen, baking, listening to music, and just being quiet sometimes, pretending to do homework while she was on the computer, doing something for the bookstore. Leah was usually still at City Hall, because the parkway fight was coming to a head. But Evie had time to sit with me that spring, when I was overflowing. She didn't even badmouth Dad much. I could tell sometimes that she wanted to, but she was on her best behavior. You had some fantastic friends, Mom.

That was the semester when I did the paper on reproductive rights in Mr. Whitaker's class. I had mostly checked out of school by then, but I got really stoked about that project. Once, when you asked how things were going at school, I told you about it. And I saw you wince. That should have been the perfect topic, in Ruth World. You had always been a champion of a woman's right to choose, her control over her own body. You had supported the clinic on St. Paul Street back in the day, when protesters tried to shut it down. I heard you had counseled some tearful students in your office. You should have been glad that I was taking such an interest. Could you tell that I wasn't going to toe the Ruth line?

Evie didn't like it. "You can't be pro-life," she said.

"Those people are Neanderthals. They just want women to stay pregnant and in the kitchen, popping out babies while the men are off at work. Or play. Or war."

"But it's a baby," I said.

"It is not a baby; it's a fetus. There's a difference." She set down her cup of tea.

"A chrysalis is the same thing as a pupa," I said. "One of them just sounds better."

She looked at me like Whoa, where did *you* come from? But she didn't say anything.

And pretty soon the school year ended, and I started hanging out with Josh, and I stopped going over to Evie and Leah's. I could sleep late, and there wasn't any homework, even for pretending. On those long summer days, 3 p.m. felt like the day was just beginning.

And you weren't watching much. When you weren't busy getting treatments, you were busy in the community garden, over in the park. You were so proud of that garden. Five years before, we had helped create it together — Dad hammering in stakes and me dropping seeds in the long rows you dug. I still have that photo of me at age ten, swamped in Dad's big floppy straw hat, with a trowel in one hand and a zucchini the size of a football in the other. It looks like I couldn't be happier.

You wanted so much from the garden — peas and kale and carrots, of course, but also an expression of our commitment to the land, where people had been growing things for centuries. You told me the history — how our whole neighborhood used to be a farm, and a hungry developer carved it up in the early 1900s, built rows of little homes for the office workers of the growing town, and named the brand new streets after his five daughters. The garden, which was open to anyone who wanted to invest a little sweat, was going to carry the whole neighborhood back to the time before that, when people still worked together on the land. So it seemed strange, Mom, when you went there every day alone, digging yourself in behind that screen of sunflowers that protected your own little plot.

I always hated that garden. I know, it was a good cause, growing things we could eat, without pesticides, without Big Ag, without supporting Exxon Mobil BP Whatever by driving the car down to the Price Chopper. But Mom, people like cars! People like supermarkets! All that stuff, the impossibly big mangos and the aisles full of bright cereal boxes, I know it's gross and unnecessary, but people like it. At least, a lot of people do. A lot of the poor people you claimed to be fighting for. In that last summer, it wasn't about those people; it was just you going to the damn garden day after day, digging yourself into oblivion.

I'll say it again: I should have known how much pain you were in. But why couldn't you tell me?

That night in July, when Josh and I put on our big boots and trampled every inch of your plot, then set the scarecrow on fire? That was the night of the Strawberry Moon. You always vibrated to all the full moons. There was something horrible about it, like dancing on Nana's grave. But there was something delicious, too.

I guess there was a perfect logic, then, to the next step. I trample your garden, you blow up my bus. So way to go, Mom. You're winning, I guess. Tough game, though, huh?

I was playing for keeps by then, because I was in love. Oh, I know you didn't think it was love—it was just a crush, on an older boy who was taking advantage of my restlessness, my eagerness. How could I be in love with a grungy dropout who smoked a lot of weed and never seemed to wash his hair or change his clothes?

Well. Were you ever in love, Mom? It may not be the most rational experience. I loved Josh *because* he didn't care about washing his hair or changing his clothes. Because he had the courage to drop out of that stupid school. Because he had the bus, and when we were in it, whispering on the mattress while the crickets sang in the night, we were a conspiracy of two against the world. Because he conjured me. Because he took me to Nectar's for gravy fries. Because because because because because.

Yes, he took off. Yes, you were right again. But don't tell me it wasn't love.

Futile—the winds—
To a heart in Port—

So. You blew up the bus, and yourself. I was in Ferrisburgh at the time, staying in an old farmhouse that was being rented by some of Josh's friends. We had left the bus for a while, because people like Mr. Marriott were getting too curious. We didn't take it out on the road any-more: Josh didn't want his friends to know it was ours; it was our little secret from the world. We parked it at the end of Louise Street, by the park. We were going to go back for it when we had saved enough money to take off for good.

And then I saw it on the local news, on somebody's computer. Professor Dies in Explosion. I watched the clip over and over. The bus — our bus — in flames, in front of the park where I used to hang by my knees from the monkey bars. Mr. and Mrs. Marriott standing by, Elly Taylor in her bathrobe, Evie and Leah, all with their hands at their sides. I never saw Elly Taylor looking so quiet.

"*There's* a school bus that won't be making any more pickups," said one of the guys at the house. Josh told him to shut up.

I was ten miles away. What could I do? Come to a memorial service? I'm sorry, but I didn't want to hear the parade of people praising you. I grew up listening to all those students you invited to the house, mostly girls, telling me, "Your mother is so cool." As if I would want to hear that. I didn't have the heart.

And I had other things on my mind. Two weeks before, I had sat in a dusty bathroom in that farmhouse and stared at two pink lines on a stick. I had seen the spotting, and felt the cramps, I had missed my period — but I still didn't believe it. I was 16. Josh was going to be furious. It was my worst nightmare. So why were the hairs on my arms standing on end?

I didn't tell Josh. I was going to take care of it. But I thought that required getting the consent of a parent. I knew you wouldn't object—you'd be eager to have it done; you'd probably get me special treatment at the clinic. But then you'd be back in my life. You'd blame it on Josh, and try to break us up. I put it off. I could feel my body ticking.

And then you blew yourself up. Now what was I supposed to do? Josh didn't say anything about the bus. Maybe he figured I just needed some time. Maybe he was terrified, like he'd get traced to it somehow. When I turned down a joint, he looked at me funny, but still— he was quiet. A plan of his own must have been taking shape in his mind. I don't know. I sleepwalked through those days.

I must have been 12 or 13 weeks when I finally acted. I needed help, but I didn't want to tell any of Josh's friends, or their girlfriends. I had left my high school friends far behind. How could they deal with this? I felt so stupid for letting it happen, for failing Sex Ed 101. I didn't have a car. But there in my phone was Evie's number.

She didn't say anything like "Fuckin' men." She hardly said anything at all. She just asked for the address and said she'd be there soon. When she arrived, she didn't ask who the father was. She just hugged me, and looked in my eyes, and beeped the car door. On the way to the clinic, she didn't play any music. Thank God: I think Adele would have killed me at that point. It was a gorgeous sunny October afternoon, the trees were bright with fall. The silence was strangely calming.

Evie had called ahead, so they were ready for me. It turned out that you don't need parental consent in Vermont. The receptionist was nice—who knows, maybe she was one of your students. The waiting room was like any doctor's office, magazines and a flat-screen TV tuned to "The Price Is Right." I signed some forms. A nurse in street clothes took me to a separate little sitting room and told me what to expect, side effects and after-care. She gave me a brochure on depression.

I put on that backless hospital "gown," and they took me into the bright little operating room. They asked me my birthdate again, and was I allergic to anything, and I said no. I crossed my legs and I said, "I mean no to all of this."

The doctor said, "Come again?" I thought that was funny. Come again? I said no, I won't be coming again. And I went back to the little dressing room, took off that stupid johnny, dressed, and walked back out to the waiting room. Evie looked up from her magazine, surprised to see me so soon. I said, "Let's go." She looked at me hard, and started to say something, and then she just got up and put on her coat. God bless Evie.

I never felt so scared, or so happy, as when we stepped out of that building. The fallen leaves glittered in the sun like bits of colored crystal.

And here it is April, and this morning, from the window of Evie and Leah's guest room, I watched the full moon setting. The Passover Moon. I wake up super early these days—it seems like I constantly need to pee. And I'm constantly hungry, too. Evie brings me fries from Nectar's, and Leah gives her dirty looks for indulging me in junk food, and then we all crack up.

I know I'm not supposed to miss Josh—fuckin' men— but I do. I think of him out on the road somewhere, or in another town—he always wanted to go to California. He's probably with another girl by now, and I just want to be her. That's how weak I am.

I've failed at almost everything, Mom. Failed to keep my father around. Failed to please my mother. Couldn't hack it in school. Didn't get invited to Francie Lampson's sleepovers. Couldn't play the freakin' piano to save my life. Couldn't hold onto Josh.

So. This is ridiculous, right? I'm an unmarried 16 year-old high school dropout, a kid about to have a kid. I hear you saying, "Harper, don't be ridiculous." And you know what I do next? I clap my hands over my ears, and I go Na na na na na na na—

THE NIGHT THE WASHINGTON GENERALS WON

My insubordination started in Roanoke. Or maybe it was Lynchburg, sometimes I didn't pay such close attention to the towns. But I remember that game, because it was the first time I threw a monkey wrench in the works of the mighty Harlem Globetrotters.

They were running the Statue of Liberty routine, the one in which Tiny Thorndike just stood at midcourt and held the ball high above his head—which was damn high, since Tiny was 7 foot 4—while all the opposing players swarmed around him, jumping and taking fruitless swipes at thin air, until finally little Mimsy Furst came scooting by, and Tiny just dropped the ball into his hands, so Mimsy could motor downcourt for an uncontested layup. The opposing players—that would be my team—threw up their arms in theatrical dismay, and the crowd roared at yet another hilarious Globetrotter score.

Except that this time, in Roanoke or Lynchburg or wherever, I didn't play along. I knew what was coming, of course: all these trick plays were carefully choreographed and rehearsed. Just before Mimsy came zipping past, I lowered my head and plowed into Tiny, wrapping my arms around his ribcage, which was about as high as I could reach. The ball squirted out of his grasp, right into the hands of one of my teammates, and the Trotters could only watch as Dombrowski laid it in the basket for us. The refs were so startled by my egregious foul that they swallowed their whistles. Meadowlark Lemon, captain of the Globetrotters, the Clown Prince of Basketball, gave me a funny look. But the clock was still ticking, so we got back to business. Of course, we still lost the game. I wasn't that lawless. Not yet.

The next day, when our bus stopped at a Stuckey's in western Virginia, I happened to encounter Meadowlark in the men's room. When I walked in, he was standing at the urinal, dressed to the nines, as usual. Dark suit, dazzling white shirt collar, sharp creases in his extra-long trousers. Seeing me over his shoulder, he hunched over dramatically and said, "Don't you get close to me, Jim." Meadowlark called everyone Jim. I said, "What are you talking about? Why are you all scrunched up like that?"

"I'm protecting my stuff, man. Every time you see something big, you wanna tackle it."

I just laughed and went about my business, but that evening I messed things up again. This time it was the Hand Grenade routine, which called for Meadowlark himself to get a rebound and then linger under the basket while the other team — that would be us — retreated to defensive positions at our own end of the court. The rest of the Trotters hustled over to their bench, eyes wide in fear, and huddled with their hands over their ears. Meadowlark brought the ball up to his mouth, bit off an invisible detonating pin, took aim downcourt, and hurled the projectile at us in a long, perfect arc. At the better arenas, they had sound effects: a whistling bomb and a blast on contact, at which point all of us pigeons fell down and one of the Trotters swooped in, scooped up the ball, and dunked it pretty as you please. Meadowlark dusted off his hands. Only this time, in Danville or wherever, when my teammates did the All Fall Down thing, I didn't. I caught the ball, put it up to my ear, made a show of hearing nothing, and heaved it back to Meadowlark. He just looked perplexed. So did my teammates. But we lost again, as usual.

After the game that night, Nickerson stopped me on my way to the showers. He looked apologetic. Nickerson always looked apologetic; it was like his face was sorry to impose itself on you. Maybe it was because he had no chin. Lots of red Irish cheeks and forehead, but no chin. He must have had a terrible time putting on a pillowcase. He wore a tatty brown suit and a matching fedora, like he was covering a New York prize fight in 1925, not a rigged basketball game in Cul de Sac, Virginia in 1971. He was the PR guy for HG Inc., and by God he had a job to do.

"Red," he said, "What was that about?"

"What?"

"The Hand Grenade! That's not how it goes."

"What, you didn't like it? I thought it was a nice little

change of pace. You know, maybe a little anti-war statement." Honestly, what with Vietnam and all, I thought
that routine wasn't in the best of taste.

"Abe isn't going to like it, Red." Nickerson looked at
his watch—he always had to report to the owner back in
Chicago after a game—and I managed to slip past him
into the locker room.

I wouldn't have known how to answer him, anyway.
I just couldn't seem to stop myself. A couple of nights
later, I'm pretty sure it was in Hickory, North Carolina,
I took it further. That was the night I broke up the dribbling routine of the magnificent Curly Neal. That's what
Nickerson always called him in the press releases—"the
magnificent Curly Neal." Maybe you've seen this bit on
TV. Curly brought the ball up the court, made his way
into a little forest of defenders—that would be us—and
started dribbling circles around them. He bobbed in and
out, handling the ball like it was attached to his fingers
with invisible filaments, leaning so close to the floor
that he seemed to be adjusting for the earth's magnetic
field. Our job was to wave at him like toreadors. One of
us—this would be me—was supposed to chase him as
he weaved among the others, all the while dribbling a
tap-dance tattoo. Meanwhile, Curly's teammates congre-
gated under the basket, leaning on invisible lampposts,
yawning histrionically, studying their manicures. Just
when it seemed that the chasing defender—again, that
would be me—was about to run him to ground, the routine called for Curly to do a one-eighty, dribble the ball

between my legs, pop past me without missing a bounce, and flip a pass to Meadowlark, who would toss it into the hoop unmolested.

It was a great bit, this little bald guy making me into his own personal Maypole. We had it all so perfectly cal-ibrated, like a fine Swiss watch, it could make you proud to be the fall guy. But that night in Hickory, I tocked when I should have ticked. At the moment of the big drib-ble-through, I closed the gate. The ball caromed off my knee into our halfcourt, and one of my teammates laid it in with ease.

Curly looked at me like I'd just cut a fart in his mama's parlor. And I admit, I didn't like messing with him. He let me borrow his Agatha Christies after he finished them, and sometimes we talked about the clues. Be-sides, he was really good at what he did; he could have played for real.

After the game, poor Nickerson looked like somebody had shot his dog. I said, "I'm sorry, Nick—I just messed up, is all. My timing's a little off lately. But hey, we lost again, right?"

He nodded, and didn't say anything. Over by the home team's bench, Meadowlark was just gazing at me.

I always had mixed feelings about Meadowlark Lemon. Yes, he was good. He worked hard at making it look easy, and you had to admire that. And he was a hell of an athlete, even in 1971, when he was in the twilight of his career and he couldn't really run anymore. He didn't need to run: on those long legs, he loped faster than some of the younger guys sprinted. Nobody knew exactly how old he was; that was part of his legend. And of course the Trotters routines were orchestrated to let him take it easy. That whole Foul-Lane Crossover bit, where he kept interrupting the opposing player who was trying to take a free throw? (That would be me, by the way.) It started one night when Meadow just needed a blow. He knew I was going to dribble three times before shooting; that was my ritual. Just after the final dribble, as I was poised to shoot, he held up his hands, shouted "Whoa!" and crossed the foul lane in front of me, to take a spot on the other side. Then he looked at me as if to say Okay, Mister Man, now you can do your thing. So I went back to my ritual, and just after the third dribble he did it again, crossing back to the other side. He made a big show of settling in there, then signaled to me to proceed, as if I was the one who was holding things up. A few minutes later, after about seven more repetitions of this bit, he had the crowd in stitches, and me in agony, and he was ready to start loping again. Our press releases always called him "the legendary Meadowlark Lemon," which was a load of hooey. But he was damn good. You never saw anybody so loose-jointed, so able to do three things at once. He could be jawing with the ref and making goo-goo eyes at a woman in the crowd and at the same time pulling off the most remarkable full-court pass, underhand, alley-oop, right to the rim.

The man was a master of the great trick of getting the audience — and the opponent — to focus on one thing while he was actually doing another.

If you're like most people, mentioning the Harlem Globetrotters probably stirs a few standard images. A team full of talented black guys in star-spangled uniforms warming up to the clickety-clack of "Sweet Georgia Brown." Trick shots and gags — the Yo-Yo Ball, the Foul Lane Crossover, the baiting and hoodwinking of the poor dumb refs. And the Trotters never lost. Never ever. Until they did. January 5, 1971, in Johnson City, Tennessee. That's what this story is about.

Of course, if they were always going to win, that meant their opponents always had to lose. So they needed a perpetual patsy — a team that traveled with them and made them look good by losing to them night after night. That was the Washington Generals. That was my team.

For the record, I should point out that the Washington Generals had nothing to do with Washington, either the city or the state. It was just a joke name, the inverse of General Washington. Sometimes, in fact, we were the New Jersey Reds, or the St. Louis Stars, or the Cleveland Zephyrs. Sometimes we were just the White Guys.

Not that it was supposed to be a racial thing. I mean, yes, the Globetrotters were all black; that was part of their identity. Back in the bad old days, when they weren't welcome in the NBA, the best black guys played for the

Trotters. That was when it was still a serious team, taking on anyone who dared to challenge them. There probably wasn't a professional team in the country that could have beaten them in a straight-up game. And I'd be lying if I said that blackness wasn't part of their mystique; even then, there were plenty of people saying that basketball was not going to be a white game for long. But the Generals, the perpetual losers, did not have to be all white. It just happened that way. Blame it on Abe Saperstein, the founder and owner, who directed everything from the front office. Blame it on me, if you like: I recruited our team. I would have signed up some black guys if I could have. But if you were a black guy, would you want to play for the team that always loses to the Harlem Globetrotters? I didn't think so.

My name is Red Klotz, and I was the player-coach of the Generals. When I signed up a guy, I made it clear that his job was to lose. Most of these kids were straight out of college, where they had been good enough to catch a basketball jones but not good enough to make the pros. Some of them still thought they might. The Generals were just a way station for those kids, a chance to make pocket money playing hoops until they figured out the next thing. When I went over our shtick, they nodded. They'd grown up watching the Globetrotters on "Wide World of Sports," and they knew the drill.

Of course, I wasn't exactly on the same level as Meadowlark and Curly. I was the king of the two-handed set shot. I know: that makes me about as cool as creamed beef on toast. Even in 1971, that shot was an antique, like those old leather helmets in football. By then, everybody was taking jump shots, or else soaring to the rim for a jaw-rattling dunk. But I was a 5 foot 10 inch Jewish guy; I did not soar. I shuffled around the periphery, lulling the other team into thinking they didn't need to cover me, and then, when the pass came to me, I gathered myself and uncoiled, propelling the ball from my chest with both hands. You may think it sounds silly—but it worked. In my prime, I hit sixty percent of my shots. You don't see any of those soaring jump shooters approach an average like that. How did I do it? I spent days in the gym, doing it over and over. As a kid in Brooklyn, I had put in countless hours on the little patch of cracked asphalt behind our apartment house, taking that shot again and again. I can still see the lines my father etched out there with white paint, progressively further from the sagging hoop as I got older. Repetition is the soul of athletic success. Dad always said, "Keep your head down, son"—and that's what he did, for fifty-three years. So did I, until that night in Johnson City.

2,495 games. Twenty-four hundred and ninety-five. That's how many the Trotters had won in a row, until that night. Put it another way: that's how many games the Washington Generals had lost in a row. Talk about a dream deferred. At roughly 125 games a year, that was twenty years of consecutive triumph—or futility, depending on your point of view. Of course, from my angle as the captain and sole remaining original member of the Generals, it was the latter. But that was my job—to lose to the Trotters. So if we did it night after night, day after day, well, in a sense it was a success, not a failure. We had mastered the art of losing.

The strangeness of that night in Tennessee began on the team bus. If you're thinking of the Trotters and the Generals as two different teams, you'd be thinking of two buses, arriving from two different places. But we played the Trotters almost every day, so of course we traveled together. It was just twenty guys, Nickerson, and a teenaged equipment manager we called Scrotum. We provided our own refs, because of course they had to be in on the choreography. They were just a couple of Generals who put on striped shirts. God knows Abe wasn't going to pay for two buses.

I haven't said much about Abe Saperstein yet — but Abe was behind it all, one way or another. He had always pinched every nickel until the buffalo bellowed, and he wasn't getting any more generous as time wore on. After all, the Trotters weren't exactly thriving. The NBA was getting all the best players now, black and white, and they were on TV every week. Who needed to come out and see a bunch of aging jokesters in stripey shorts? Our crowds kept dwindling. And the smaller the crowds got, the more Abe made us play. I mean, if your profit margin on the widget shrinks, what do you do? You sell more widgets.

That's why we were playing in Johnson City. Tennessee. On a week night. In a high school gym. And not one of the better high schools, I might add. We, who once played on the deck of the U.S.S. Nimitz, with Eisenhower in the front row and Mamie Van Doren tossing up the opening jump ball. You should have seen how she filled out a zebra shirt. But here we were in Dick Town, as Tiny Thorndike called it ("Get it?" he said, "Johnson City?"), four days after New Year's, playing for a bunch of yahoos who didn't know a pick and roll from a pirouette.

So we were all on the same bus, with the Trotters in the back, as usual. I know what you're thinking: back of the bus. But it wasn't a racial thing. Or it was, but not in that way. Those guys wanted the back. It was like a school bus, where the cool kids all sat together — and the farther from the front, the better. Nickerson took the first seat on the right, so he could check off our names on a clipboard as we got on. Us Generals clustered behind him, wishing we could sit in the back, too. Don't get me wrong, nobody said we couldn't. But we didn't, that's just the way it was.

It was snowing, a fine, dry snow that ticked on the windshield. Gracie hit the wipers from time to time, but they didn't do much good.

We all loved Gracie, who had driven the bus forever. She had an Elvira Gulch look — a long, lozenge-shaped face, and a long nose, too, with a substantial bump like it had been broken when she was a kid but they couldn't afford to fix it. Black hair, and dark eyes that never seemed to settle on anything, except when she was driving. When she was driving, she was all business. If she thought it was strange to be the only female on that busload of steaming testosterone, she never showed it. I bet she grew up with brothers. Maybe she just loved the smell of Aqua Velva. The guys treated her with the utmost respect, like the mother of some girl they wanted to get with. And Nickerson chatted at her ceaselessly.

"Ever been to Johnson City, Gracie?"

"Nope." She was straining to see through the blowing snow.

"Bet they don't get a lot of snow here. Probably don't have much in the way of snow plows. You know these small towns in the south: an inch of snow can paralyze the whole place for days. Of course, they don't get enough snow to make it a priority."

The snow surged more thickly on the windshield. Nickerson went on.

"Still, when you need a snowplow, you need a snowplow."

"Yep." It wasn't that Gracie was incommunicative. If you sat with her at a truck stop while the guys were filling up on burgers and soggy pizza, she could talk like nobody's business. She had a deep raspy voice that just made you long for a cigarette. I had been trying to quit for months; sometimes I sat with her just for her smoker's breath. She always carried a paperback novel for the long waits while we were practicing or playing, and I liked to ask her about the plots. On that trip she was working on one called *My Lord Savage*. It was about this Iroquois chieftain named Silver Otter whose wife and children

had been slaughtered by settlers, and he had vowed revenge, but then he was captured during a raid, and while
in captivity he fell in love with Rowena Churchill, the
governor's beautiful but innocent daughter, who was en-
thralled by his dark smoldering eyes and his primitive
passion...you get the idea. I could listen to Gracie tell
those stories all day long.

I don't know how she put up with Nickerson, though.
The man just wouldn't shut up.

"If this snow continues," he said, "This town is gonna
be a mess."

Gracie just nodded and kept driving.The strange thing
was, the back of the bus was silent. Usually, there would
be music on Tiny Thorndike's transistor radio — I swear,
Tiny could find a soul station in Siberia — and lots of chatter, playing the dozens, rueful abuse of those two girls at
the refreshment stand the night before. But on that day
there was nothing but static. Everybody seemed trans-
fixed by the falling snow.

People have asked: What was I thinking when I made
that shot? Didn't I know I was supposed to miss it?

Of course I knew. I may be an ornery SOB, but I'm not
stupid.

The thing is, that game was different. Right from the
jump, you could feel it. When the Trotters warmed up
without "Sweet Georgia Brown," I figured somebody had
just lost the tape, or maybe that tacky gym didn't have a

sound system. But then in the first half the Trotters didn't do The Hand Grenade. Or The Bowling Ball. Or The Man from Triberica, with the robotic alien dribble straight to the hoop. Meadowlark didn't jaw at the refs, or make small talk with the women in the front row. He didn't chase Dombrowski into the stands with a plumber's helper.

Instead, the Trotters were playing basketball. Curly brought the ball up and ran an actual offense, and they played a little real defense, too. I'd never seen the Trotters play defense; it seemed downright un-American.

And they were killing us. They were getting basket after easy basket, and we were completely discombobulated, because our dance partner refused to dance. My guys looked at me. When I brought the ball up the floor at the end of the half, I looked at Meadowlark. He clapped his hands and said, "Bring it."

At halftime, Dombrowski, this big Polish kid with a pornstar mustache, asked what we should do. Should we make some shots? And maybe play some defense, too? I said, "We should bring it."

And that second half, we brang it. That was the best the Generals ever played. It was like a pick-up game back in Bed-Stuy: guys were setting screens, boxing out, playing some serious D. The refs (who were two of our guys, after all) were letting us play, not calling fouls unless we drew blood. Dombrowski had a field day under the basket: he was way quicker than Tiny Thorndike, who moved like he was made out of Tinker Toys. I made some bombs from outside, and we whittled away at the Trotters' lead. That's why, at the end, it was close enough for my final shot to matter: with seven seconds left, I hit a twenty-footer that gave us our first lead of the game.

But seven seconds, as the broadcasters love to tell you, is an eternity at the end of a game. Time enough for everything to be set right, for down to become up again. Time for Meadowlark to take his own final shot, the real final shot. All he had to do was make it, and the crowd would have gone home happy. The Trotters would have won yet again, little boys would still love Wheaties, and all would be right with the world. If you had ever seen Meadowlark in a shoot-around, or just messing around in the gym—he loved taking a guy's per diem in a ruthless game of Horse—you knew: if he took that shot ten times, he made it eleven.

But no. The legendary Meadowlark Lemon sent his buzzer-beating shot clanging off the rim. It wasn't even close. Dombrowski raised his arms in triumph—and then looked around uncertainly, and lowered them. The crowd sat in silence. Then somebody booed, a low baritone, like a ghost of unhappiness. Standing behind the Globetrotters' bench, Nickerson looked like the sky had fallen. And then people just started filing out. Didn't they know what they'd seen? They should have been rioting, demanding their money back. Those were strange days.

So I made the damn shot, and Meadowlark missed his, and the Generals won. I got the hell out of there without even taking a shower. I didn't want to deal with Nickerson's dismay. I knew what I'd done. If I got on the bus, people would ask me questions I wouldn't know how to answer. So I tossed my duffle bag to Scrotum, pulled up the collar of my trench coat, and started walking. How lost could I get in Johnson City, Tennessee?

Snow was still falling. Nickerson was right about one thing: the whole town seemed paralyzed. Not that I minded; I wasn't looking for company. I just wanted to walk. I got off the main drag and tromped through a residential neighborhood, where the only sign of life was the occasional porch light. In three inches of slushy snow, my sneakers got thoroughly soaked. I didn't care. I just walked.

At one point I happened on a phone booth at a corner, its light like a beacon on a watch hill. I stepped in and dialed the number in Brooklyn. It was going to be a collect call, but I wasted my time wondering if she would accept the charges. It just rang.

Eventually I found my way back to the motel, where our bus hulked in the parking lot. Poor Nickerson probably had a fit when I wasn't on it after the game. The sky was still dark, but the motel coffee shop was open, lights glowing on the snowy pavement. I went in. The bus would be pulling out by 8 a.m.; might as well make it an all-nighter now.

It was one of those cheerful fake-diner places with gleaming chrome walls, red leatherette booths, and matching red stools at the counter. Framed newspaper reviews from 1958. Metal pedestals on the formica by the cash register, with doughnuts and pies under clear plastic covers. From the kitchen beyond the counter came the tinny sound of a radio playing scratchy pop music. And there, in a booth facing the door, watching me enter, was the legendary Meadowlark Lemon.

He was dressed, as always, impeccably. Gray suit with wide lapels, spotless white shirt with a broad collar and a shiny burgundy tie. Matching pocket square. I became freshly aware of my soggy, rumpled trench coat and the damp sweat suit beneath it. He gestured with a huge dark hand to the bench facing him. What could I do? I slid in.

"Who knew there was a five o'clock in the morning too, eh, Jim?" He laughed that big braying laugh of his. I lifted a laminated menu from between the napkin holder and the sugar dispenser. Ice water squelched in my tube socks.

"What are you doing up, Meadow?"

"Oh, havin' some pie, is all," he said, pointing to his plate. "I don't sleep like I used to. And the pie is surprisingly good."

We were the only customers, and the only waitress came over, a chunky white girl with a half-apron over her jeans. She looked like she might have this job for the next forty years. I ordered coffee, and she filled up a white melmac mug. I poured in two packets of sweetener and three creamers. Meadowlark watched with a little smile.

"That stuff'll kill you, Jim."

"Well," I said, "at least I'll die caffeinated." I found a cigarette in the trench coat's inner chest pocket, and pulled it out. "Don't tell me this will stunt my growth."

"It'll stunt your growth, Jim. Don't say I didn't tell you." He laughed. Then he said, "You look like something the cat drug in. After the cat finished messin' with it."

I lit up. The cigarette was impossibly good. "I couldn't sleep either," I said. "I've got this problem with my toe."

"Your toe."

"Yeah, my big toe. It's got this raw spot that throbs, you know? I mean, I don't even notice until I go to bed, and then it rubs against the sheets and it hurts like hell."

"So you go walkin' in the snow?"

"It doesn't bother me when I'm moving."

"Yeah, that makes sense." He rolled his eyes. "I been tellin' you, Jim, it's those cheap-ass canvas sneakers you insist on wearin'." Meadowlark loved his new Adidas. "Just because Tommy Heinsohn wears them, that doesn't make them good for your feet. Au contraire."

"You sound like my father."

"Yeah?"

"He said everything starts with a good pair of shoes."

"Well, then he wasn't always wrong." He took a bite of pie. After a minute, he said, "Sounds like you got white folks' problems, Jim."

"Excuse me?"

"You know how many boys on my team even knew they daddies?"

"No."

He did the mental rolodex. "Three. Know how many are glad they knew they daddies?"

I shook my head.

"One. On a good day." He laughed a big laugh. "Not that I know anything about your father. Maybe he was a right sonofabitch. But you got the air of a man who knew his father."

"What is this, psychotherapy?"

"You see a couch in here? This is just two guys talkin'." Then he gave me a quizzical look. "Where's that woman of yours, Jim?"

What could I say? I thought I'd try the truth. "She's not coming back," I said.

He grunted, deep and low. Then he said, "You know what else ain't comin' back?"

I shrugged.

"Your youth. Your knees. Your ability to score three times in one night." He laughed. "Remember that? Man, I do." He sucked his teeth. "It's the way of the world, Jim. But they ain't no use cryin' in your oatmeal."

I took a drag from my cigarette. God, it was good. "Meadow, why do you keep doing this?"

He looked me square in the eyes. "I got debts, Jim. A credit card is a crazy-ass thing." He laughed. "Plus," he started counting items on his long yellow fingers, "I got alimony. Times two. What was I thinking?" Another laugh, another finger. "Plus, child support. I got to do my part for little Wilt and Billie. And Oscar." He shook his head. "Bad enough that I'm on the road all the time. I got to stay legendary, Jim. Got to stay legendary." He looked out the window, then back at me. "Also?" Another finger. "I like makin' people laugh. So sue me."

He took a sip of coffee, and went on. "But maybe you haven't messed up like I have. Maybe you could just walk away."

I nodded.

"I got to tell you, Jim, we'd miss you something fierce. Nobody chases Curly like you do. Look like somebody set your hair on fire."

I smiled.

"And nobody does the Foul Lane thing like you. Remember when we tried Farley on that? Boy couldn't dribble three times and pause to save his mama's life." He laughed. "But you, Jim, you like Philly Joe Jones ridin' the high hat. I could interrupt you with my eyes closed. Yeah, we'd miss you."

He took a bite of pie, and inspected the tines of his fork. "Tell you what, Red."

That got my attention.

"Let's throw for it."

"What?"

"Rock Paper Scissors."

"You're kidding."

Meadow just looked at me. Then he held out a fist. After a beat, so did I.

Juke, juke, throw.

I knew he'd go Rock. So why'd I throw Scissors?

There was a long pause while he took a last bite of pie. On the radio, Sly and the Family Stone were smart-alecking their way through "Thank You." I finally asked him the question.

"Meadow, did you miss that shot on purpose?"

"What shot? I take a shitload of shots, Jim, you might have noticed that about me. I'm the biggest gunner in" — he looked around the coffee shop—"Tennessee, right? But that's what they pay me for. I figure if I miss a few, it helps my boys with their offensive rebound statistics."

"You know what shot."

"Oh, that shot."

I just looked at him. He went on.

"See, now, you had just made a shot, right? And it was a beauty, by the way. I don't know where you got that funky-ass set shot—did your daddy teach you that?"

I nodded.

"Well, it looks like a cat coughin' up a hairball—but it gets the job done. Gets the job done." He took a sip of coffee. "So you had just made that shot, and I've got what, eight seconds—"

"Seven."

"Who's tellin' this story? And you guys put one man on me? Dombrowski? That's just a insult, Jim. I could beat Dombrowski with two hands behind my back. So maybe I was a little nonchalant." He said this with a French flourish. "Anyhow, I didn't want to make it too early, give you another chance, who knows what you'd do. Have a existential breakdown or somethin'."

I didn't say anything.

"So maybe I dogged it a little. I mean, I'm supposed to make it look easy, right? I am the legendary Meadowlark Lemon!" He barked a big laugh. "And I been makin' that shot all my life. Nothin' to get all het up about."

He took another sip of coffee. "But you know, Jim, sometimes you miss. Sometimes you miss."

He signaled to the waitress, who came over quickly. "Pearl," he said, "Get this man some pie."

She nodded brightly. Her name tag said "Judy."

Meadowlark got up. "One thing for damn sure," he said. "I get a chance at that shot tonight, it's goin' down." He put a ten on the table. "I'll be sorry to spoil your win streak, Jim." He laughed. "But that'll be one in a row for us." He straightened his tie and loped off.

He was right: the pie was surprisingly good. I asked for more coffee, and watched the wan daylight rise on the parking lot. The snow was already melting. People started coming in. I quit smoking again, for real.

After a while I heard a familiar voice, and looked up to see Nickerson by the "Please Wait To Be Seated" sign. He was nattering on as usual. But what was Gracie doing there with him? At seven a.m.? I did a double-take. Gracie just smiled.

Fomite

A fomite is a medium capable of transmitting infectious organisms from one individual to another.

"The activity of art is based on the capacity of people to be infected by the feelings of others." Tolstoy, *What Is Art?*

Writing a review on Amazon, Good Reads, Shelfari, Library Thing or other social media sites for readers will help the progress of independent publishing. To submit a review, go to the book page on any of the sites and follow the links for reviews. Books from independent presses rely on reader to reader communications.

For more information or to order any of our books, visit
http://www.fomitepress.com/FOMITE/Our_Books.html

Nothing Beside Remains
Jaysinh Birjépatil

The Way None
of This Happened
Mike Breiner

Summer on the
Cold War Planet
Paula Closson Buck

Foreign Tales of
Exemplum and Woe
J. C. Ellefson

Free Fall/Caída libre
Tina Escaja

Speckled Vanities
Marc Estrin

Fomite

Off to the Next Wherever
John Michael Flynn

Derail This Train Wreck
Daniel Forbes

Semitones
Derek Furr

Where There Are Two or More
Elizabeth Genovise

The Three Lives of Jonathan Force
Richard Hawley

In A Family Way
Zeke Jarvis

A Rising Tide of People Swept Away
Scott Archer Jones

A Free, Unsullied Land
Maggie Kast

Shadowboxing With Bukowski
Darrell Kastin

Fomite

Feminist on Fire
Coleen Kearon

Thicker Than Blood
Jan English Leary

*A Guide
to the Western Slopes*
Roger Lebovitz

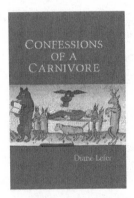

Confessions of a Carnivore
Diane Lefer

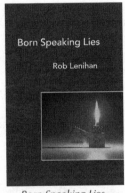

Born Speaking Lies
Rob Lenihan

*Unborn Children of
America*
Michele Markarian

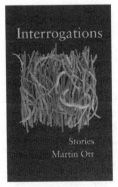

Interrogations
Martin Ott

*Connecting the Dots
to Shangrila*
Joseph D. Reich

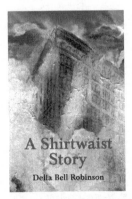

Shirtwaist
Delia Bell Robinson

Fomite

Isles of the Blind
Robert Rosenberg

What We Do For Love
Ron Savage

Bread & Sentences
Peter Schumann

Principles of Navigation
Lynn Sloan

A Great Fullness
Bob Sommer

Industrial Oz
Scott T. Starbuck

Among Angelic Orders
Susan Thoma

Industrial Oz
Scott T. Starbuck

*The Inconveniece
of the Wings*
Silas Dent Zobal

Fomite

More Titles from Fomite...

Joshua Amses — *Raven or Crow*

Joshua Amses — *The Moment Before an Injury*

Jaysinh Birjepatel — *The Good Muslim of Jackson Heights*

Antonello Borra — *Alfabestiario*

Antonello Borra — *AlphaBetaBestiaro*

Jay Boyer — *Flight*

David Brizer — *Victor Rand*

David Cavanagh — *Cycling in Plato's Cave*

Dan Chodorkoff — *Loisada*

Michael Cocchiarale — *Still Time*

James Connolly — *Picking Up the Bodies*

Greg Delanty — *Loosestrife*

Catherine Zobal Dent — *Unfinished Stories of Girls*

Mason Drukman — *Drawing on Life*

Zdravka Evtimova — *Carts and Other Stories*

Zdravka Evtimova — *Sinfonia Bulgarica*

Anna Faktorovich — *Improvisational Arguments*

Derek Furr — *Suite for Three Voices*

Stephen Goldberg — *Screwed and Other Plays*

Barry Goldensohn — *The Hundred Yard Dash Man*

Barry Goldensohn — *The Listener Aspires to the Condition of Music*

R. L. Green When — *You Remember Deir Yassin*

Greg Guma — *Dons of Time*

Andrei Guriuanu — *Body of Work*

Ron Jacobs — *All the Sinners Saints*

Fomite

Ron Jacobs — *Short Order Frame Up*

Ron Jacobs — *The Co-conspirator's Tale*

Kate MaGill — *Roadworthy Creature, Roadworthy Craft*

Tony Magistrale — *Entanglements*

Gary Miller — *Museum of the Americas*

Ilan Mochari — *Zinsky the Obscure*

Jennifer Anne Moses — *Visiting Hours*

Sherry Olson — *Four-Way Stop*

Andy Potok — *My Father's Keeper*

Janice Miller Potter — *Meanwell*

Jack Pulaski — *Love's Labours*

Charles Rafferty — *Saturday Night at Magellan's*

Joseph D. Reich — *The Hole That Runs Through Utopia*

Joseph D. Reich — *The Housing Market*

Joseph D. Reich — *The Derivation of Cowboys and Indians*

Kathryn Roberts — *Companion Plants*

David Schein — *My Murder and Other Local News*

Peter Schumann — *Planet Kasper, Volumes One and Two*

Fred Skolnik — *Rafi's World*

Lynn Sloan — *Principles of Navigation*

L.E. Smith — *The Consequence of Gesture*

L.E. Smith — *Views Cost Extra*

L.E. Smith — *Travers' Inferno*

Susan Thomas — *The Empty Notebook Interrogates Itself*

Tom Walker — *Signed Confessions*

Sharon Webster — *Everyone Lives Here*

Susan V. Weiss — *My God, What Have We Done?*

Tony Whedon — *The Tres Riches Heures*

Fomite

Tony Whedon — *The Falkland Quartet*

Peter M. Wheelwright — As It Is On Earth

Suzie Wizowaty —The Return of Jason Green

35737825R00136

Made in the USA
Middletown, DE
13 October 2016